Five Photos o

AGNÈS DESARTHE is the author o. ̦̦ ̦ ̦ ̦ ̦,
Un secret sans importance and *Quelques minutes du bonheur absolu*.
Five Photos of My Wife is her first book to be published in English.
She lives in Paris with her husband, a filmmaker, and children.

ADRIANA HUNTER works as a translator from French into English. Her previous translation was Geneviève Jurgensen's *The
Disappearance*. She lives in Norfolk with her husband and children.

from the reviews of the French edition:

'From the memories of an old man, Agnès Desarthe has carved out
a novel of irresistible charm. It is sober, tender, moving, underpinned
by the disorienting wit of the hero Max, and haunted by his unforget-
table wife Telma. Desarthe is a master at expressing the unspeakable
truths of daily life and of time passing.'   *Madame Figaro*

'You'll laugh, you'll cry, you'll crumple before this terrifically affect-
ing book, a book full of life. In rubbing up against the old man and
the young artists, you'll feel like one of their number, you'll even
fancy yourself for one of Desarthe's offspring.'
                                            Journal du Dimanche

'A fine and sensitive writer, Desarthe glides with wit around the
octogenarian stranded with his memories. She knows exactly how
people talk of the small things, fleeting pleasures or invisible injuries,
that end up constituting the very essence of a human life.'
                                                        Télérama

'In a deft and dancing style, Desarthe captures the gravity of those
who live alone on the ruins of their past, getting sadder and sadder.
From such unkempt lives, the novelist pulls melancholy, enchanting
tales – full of wit and lyricism – that offer all the relief of a soothing
balm on a severe burn.'   *Magazine Littéraire*

'Agnès Desarthe has the ability to address the most serious of matters in the lightest, simplest fashion ... in the great tradition of Isaac Bashevis Singer.'   *L'Express*

'Desarthe's writing pleasingly mixes irony, sensitivity and delicacy. She has Reality undress before us, and invents sweet fables that mull memorably over love, ageing and memory.'   *Marie France*

'Desarthe gives us a series of tart sketches, dusted with satire and dark, dark comedy.'   *Aujourd'hui le Parisien*

'A meditation, amongst other things, on amorous idolatry, on the mysteries of death, and on the power and untrustworthiness of images.'   *L'Officiel*

'Tells its story with humour, with freshness, with total finesse.'
Midi Libre

'At once sombre and sprightly'   *Nice-Matin*

'Great writing that holds its fond gaze on an individual whom, in getting old, has lost none of his capacity to enjoy the fragile riches of the emotions.'   *Le Matin*

'The book is moving, but not at all sad. The old man has much by way of spirit and wit. And his creator has the skill to deal gracefully with the weightiest of themes.'   *Le Soir Illustré*

'Desarthe is a kind of spy of letters'   *Elle*

Agnès Desarthe

Five Photos of My Wife

Translated from the French by Adriana Hunter

Flamingo
An Imprint of HarperCollins*Publishers*

Flamingo
An Imprint of HarperCollins*Publishers*
77–85 Fulham Palace Road,
Hammersmith, London w6 8jb

Flamingo is a registered trade mark
of HarperCollins*Publishers* Limited

www.**fire**and**water**.com

Published by Flamingo 2001
1 3 5 7 9 8 6 4 2

First published in France as *Cinq Photos de Ma Femme*
by Editions de L'Olivier 1998

Copyright © Agnès Desarthe 1998

English translation copyright © Adriana Hunter 2001

Agnès Desarthe asserts the moral right to
be identified as the author of this work

Adriana Hunter asserts the moral right to
be identified as the translator of this work

The publication of this book is supported by the
Cultural Service of the French Embassy in London

institut français

A catalogue record for this book
is available from the British Library

ISBN 0 00 710091 4

Set in Minion by
Rowland Phototypesetting Ltd, Bury St Edmunds, Suffolk

Printed and bound in Great Britain by
Clays Ltd, St Ives plc

Five Photos of My Wife

Max

Max had been known as Mathusalem for a long time. It was the name that his mother had given him. At first, people had made fun of it, saying that he was sweet but old before his time. She laughed along with them and said: 'He'll bury us all!'

She was the first to confirm her prediction. A week before Mathusalem's third birthday, she died of blood poisoning.

As soon as he was old enough to choose for himself, the rebellious son lost no time in dropping his cumbersome first name. In 1933, having just arrived from Russia, he told the French registrar that his name was Max and he added, less out of respect for his late mother than for fear of waking her rage from beyond the grave, that Mathusalem was his second name.

Sixty years later, at eighty, he still had all his hair, which he wore long, and he felt he still had the vigour of a young man. When his wife Telma had died the previous year, he had found himself in the cemetery, stupefied, barely understanding what he was doing there. The months passed without bringing him the least enlightenment. When the spring came round again, he had spent hours at a time sitting on a bench in the park watching the buds on the trees. The tiny leaves, soft green tending towards yellow, emerged as pointed arrows before spreading themselves out. Who would have believed a few weeks earlier that the dry, black twigs would be covered in flowers? Death didn't exist.

19th April 1994

My darling,

Some news from your old father Max.

How are you? Yesterday I was at the Chinese restaurant and I thought of you. Do you remember the paper parasols that they put in the ice-creams? So prettily made. I think they're painted by hand. I turned it over in my fingers and I thought of you. Don't mention it to Marumi San, your illustrious husband; he'll go saying that I think he's Chinese again. But tell me, darling, just between you and me, it's true that Japan and China are quite similar, isn't it? They're both a long way away, anyway.

Right, I'll stop complaining. You know I can't stand people feeling sorry for me. I went to Zac's wife's funeral incognito. Dark glasses, pin-stripe suit, very elegant. I didn't want them all queuing up to see me, Lili, Boris, Victor, and the whole gang coming to say: 'And what about you, poor Max? It's not even a year since Telma left you.'

Left me, what's that supposed to mean? She's vanished into thin air is more like it. You know that hippie of a brother of yours hates me making jokes about your mother's cremation? It's odd though, isn't it? He would never listen to anything, even as a child. He's as stubborn as a mule. But as soon as I say a word against my good lady wife he gets in a complete state. Anyway, it went well, and the Association of Former Deportees were there. Zac had written a poem that was quite, quite beautiful.

How are the four of you? Send me some recent photos of the little ones. The little ones who've become big. Time passes, it passes so quickly, and you're so far away. I know I only have to take a plane. But, it's funny, I don't think I'll ever be able to do it. Like

4

when you took your first steps. I was sitting in the armchair and your mother was holding you between her knees on the window seat. I held my arms towards you and I said 'Come on, come on, my little duckling.' You only had to go a few yards. We lived in just one room. It was like a sardine tin in there. You looked at me, with your little mouth all screwed up. You were so afraid to leave your mother's arms. Now it's my turn to be frightened. The world turned upside down. It's so easy for you, you young people, to take a plane, but for me it's a complete saga.

Well, anyway. Do remember to send me some photos. Everything's fine here. I'm keeping myself busy. I go to the club, I have my bridge partners, the market twice a week, a bit of television in the evenings, but not too much. You know, after midnight there's nothing but filth. Erotic stuff, but it's so badly done, absolute rubbish. Actually, I've had very little time to myself in the last few days because of the saga of my watch. Did I tell you about my watch? A watch that worked without a hitch for thirty years. Can you believe it, suddenly, about a month ago, it went completely off the rails. I didn't realise straight away. It was losing three minutes a day. Three minutes is nothing but by the end of the week it was a good quarter of an hour. The other day, I said. 'Shall we have another game before closing time?' (this was in the club three weeks ago) and the boys all looked at me in astonishment. 'Max, it's already six o'clock,' they said. I looked at my watch: twenty to six! I spoke to my neighbour about it (he's a good man, used to be a managing director), he tells me he knows a very good watchmaker at the shopping centre. It takes me all morning to find the way in to the car park.

I asked the watchmaker if it would be worth having it repaired. It was excellent quality, automatic winding, waterproof, not just any old rubbish. I explained the whole thing to him and he told me it would cost four hundred francs, but that, for that price, he would change the glass and the winding mechanism. You know I don't like throwing money out of the window. But a good watch can cost you thousands of francs, and even then there's no guarantee that it'll work. So I said yes. He keeps it for ten days and gives it back as good as new with a year's guarantee, the whole shebang. I don't think anything more of it, but after a while I realise that it's gone completely off the rails. One day it's gaining time, the next it's losing, a disaster. I speak to my neighbour about it (the one who recommended the watchmaker), and, because he knows that it's a major expedition for me to go to the shopping centre, he goes himself (I said he was a good man). And you will never guess what that crook had to say to him: 'It's an automatic watch, you have to shake your arm to wind it up.' Can you believe that? If he's a watchmaker then I'm the Queen of England. For thirty years I didn't have to shake my arm and I never had a problem. Now he wants me to give myself another coronary by waving my arms around from morning till night.

Would you believe that one of my bridge partners is a retired jeweller? I tell him my story and he explains that I need to change some small part which only costs 5F 90. In the meantime, I've chucked four hundred francs out of the window when nowadays you can pick up a watch that works like a Seiko for just a hundred francs.

The whole business really took it out of me but, well, it's sorted out now. I don't even know why I'm telling you all this. That's all the news there is from your old father. Write when you have the time. I know you're very busy with Mariko's studies and the escapades of that rascal of a son.

A big hug for you
My regards to Marumi San
A kiss for each of my grandchildren

Your old Max.

Too late. As he drew his fingers back out of the opening in the letter box, Max realised that he had forgotten to tell his daughter the most important thing. He contemplated the little lock for a moment. He'd broken more than one of those during the war, while he was a prisoner. It couldn't be that difficult. He looked around. A traffic warden was booking someone just an arm's length away. He spat on the ground and renounced his sabotage.

After throwing a last glance at the letter box, he pulled up the collar of his jacket and asked himself why it was so difficult to write. It was more than six months since he had held Nadya in his arms. Both his children had chosen to live abroad. And why not? An adventurer's offspring can't stay put, it's a law of nature. When you really thought about it, distance didn't change any- thing. Talking to your children was like making yourself under- stood in another language. He was never sure they'd grasped what he was saying. If he told his daughter about his project, she would probably dissuade him from going through with it.

Nadya was suspicious of anything new. She liked everything to be well ordered, to be finished with, she didn't like having to go back over things. She spent her time drawing lines under columns of figures, and congratulated herself on systematically totting them up correctly. Poor little chicken, she had no idea what it felt like to lose your other half. Telma (what a brilliant woman!) had actually arranged things so that there was nothing to go back to – but her place, her outline, was still there, like a stencil on reality.

He felt her everywhere in the house, sensed her presence in the slightest draught, read messages in the furrows on the butter. Recently he had even come to wonder whether he should throw away crumbs, in case Telma's soul had taken refuge in them. She tormented him in a thousand and one ways. The more time went by, the more his every move was hampered by the invisible threads that his wife had secretly woven all through her life. The day that he broke her favourite cup when he was doing the washing-up, he put his hands up to protect his head, like a child afraid of being smacked.

'Am I possessed?' he asked himself one day. Having found no answer to this question, he decided on a counter-attack.

He would commission a painting. Telma's face painted by an artist. It would be a lovely tribute to her and a concrete way of making her understand that he accepted her new kind of presence.

There were too many photographs. Boxes full of them. And Telma was never the main subject of any of them.

He had to choose the most revealing ones to act as models. With his glasses on the end of his nose, he spread the snapshots over the table. Each image marked out life like a milestone. The time left to run could be calculated from the number of teeth, the number of wrinkles. Seen retrospectively, the least shadow under the eyes looks like a warning sign. Faces frozen in time live on in complete ignorance of their own disappearance, so distant that they pay no attention to it, so close at hand that they prefer to ignore it. The years go by, the promises become predictions and it is hard to avoid nostalgia.

After an hour Max had chosen five portraits.

Telma looking dishevelled in her kitchen as she fried meatballs. In the foreground the devastating smile of a ten-year-old Nadya and the dark eyes of Lord Byron, her eight-year-old younger brother, who had acquired this nickname thanks to his romantic poses and his way of gazing into the middle distance; Lord Byron, whose real name was Basile, his Bolivian hippie.

Ten years later: the beach at Le Touquet and in the bottom left-hand corner, tiny in the distance, Telma and her best friend Lisette, arm in arm, huddled together, each holding her hat on with her free hand – the two women's ample silhouettes forming the outline of a vase with handles.

Last year at the Association's reunion banquet, a table full of old men most of whom he had known as children somewhere on the shores of the Black Sea, Telma pulling a face as she sniffs her glass of champagne, her head haloed by a powdery cloud of white hair.

Retracing time to Nadya's university viva. Him and her, Max with his chin raised, bold and emotional, Telma turning slightly away from the camera, her long fingers partially masking her incredulous expression.

Their thirtieth wedding anniversary, at the foot of a pyramid, Telma is in a white dress and is smiling (and that's very rare) at the Egyptian guide who was speaking to her in English; she couldn't understand a word he was saying, but she had fallen in love with his camel because it had the most beautiful eyes in the world.

Telma did not look at the lens once. Max thought she was fiendish and that she had carefully avoided having her portrait taken. Now that she was no longer there to protest, he took pleasure in the idea of fixing her once and for all, of capturing her pretty triangular face in a golden frame and of spending hours in her motionless company talking in silence.

In the meantime, he often settled himself on the sitting-room sofa opposite a little oil painting of a Slav peasant woman whose rounded cheeks were accentuated by the brown and purple tones of the shawl that she wore over her head. She wore her scarf the way Telma did, or was it the other way round? Max remembered the endless arguments between his wife and Lisette about the best way of knotting a scarf. He drummed his fingers on the arm of the sofa and pulled a face.

He had never cried, even as a baby. What a memory! Telma

didn't believe him, but he could remember events that had occurred before his third birthday. And even earlier. Sometimes pictures would come back to him, so clear even though they seemed to belong to another century, an age of horses, pigs, rags, twigs and earthenware jars. In this little prehistoric universe bodies were either entirely naked or bundled into several layers of clothing, forks were a rarity compared to spoons, carts jogged along over the tracks, and people lived together with their animals. Max never cried. He knitted his eyebrows and bit his upper lip.

But, a week earlier, when he had been sitting in the same place and had felt the first tear of his life struggling to take shape in the corner of his right eye, he had made his decision. A tear of lead, solidified by so many years. More salt than water, like a minute Dead Sea.

He would have her portrait painted, oil on canvas exactly the same size as the picture in the sitting-room, with a gilt frame, no frills, something sober and elegant. It only remained for him to find the artist.

Max loved everything modern, venerated his telephone, mollycoddled his television, was eternally grateful for his central heating. With the Yellow Pages open on his knee, he set out to find the entry for painters, *see Artists and Painters.*

There were more than three pages of them. He ran through the list a first time. Two or three names caught his eye. Let chance take its course, he thought. Being methodical was all very well, but in an emergency you had to be prepared to use whatever means were available.

Di Stefano Valeria, artist, 33 rue des Martyrs, 75009.

Sober and beautiful. Simply 'artist', no fuss. Rue des Martyrs, a bit Christian sounding, but then why not. Actually, Max was mainly thinking that with a name like that it could only possibly

mean that she was a beautiful Italian woman, Silvana Mangano
in *Bitter Rice* at least.

*Gâté Gérard, teacher, qualified at the Beaux-Arts de Paris, 23
rue du Fer-à-Moulin, 75005.*

Excellent pedigree, thought Max, a teacher, you could trust
him, and the rue du Fer-à-Moulin was just round the corner
from his bridge club.

O'Donnell Angus, 13 rue des Cinq-Diamants, 75013.

Nothing to say. Ideal area. Just one stop from him on the
Metro. It was very pretty that part of the 13th Arrondissement;
perfect for a painter. And at least he had discretion to his credit
this one, no showing off of his qualifications. O'Donnell, that
was an Irish name.

Ireland. The children away in a holiday camp, a fortnight just
to themselves. Telma wanted to go to Israel with the money from
the Germans. Max had chosen Ireland. They had argued the
whole time. Morning, noon and night. The rooms in the little
guest house were poorly heated, and there was plenty of food
but Telma didn't like the taste that seemed to be everywhere.
'Mutton fat, I think,' she said with an expression of disgust, 'even
in the bread rolls.' Angry and belligerent, they watched night fall
over the lake in a dazzling wealth of colour. One evening Max
had turned his head towards Telma. He had seen her long dark
lashes shimmering in the pink light. She had installed herself on
the bank, her knees bent up to her chest, encircled by her arms,
and she was staring at the horizon, indestructible. He had watched
her admiringly. Without being able to tell her so, he had thought
then that she was a stubborn and very beautiful woman, his
cherry stone. His arms aching with the urge to hold her close,
he had forced himself to look away. It was a competition. Neither
of them was ready to give in.

Waltz Irma, 35 rue Boulard, 75014.

A German name. Mustn't be racist. All right then, Irma it is. *Irma la douce,* he sang to himself.

Zetlaoui Etienne, 6 rue des Couronnes, 75020.

Couronnes, that was in a poor area. When you're short of money, you work much harder. Max knew all about that.

At the time of the Liberation he had done all sorts of little jobs: porter at the Halles; messenger; painter and decorator. Telma worked in the rag trade for the Steiners. They ran a large workshop and would have taken Max on happily, but he had already sworn he would not succumb to that. His father had been a tailor and he remembered him bent double from morning till night, altering trousers that no longer fitted, transforming the mother's wedding dress into pillow cases for the daughter's trousseau.

Nevertheless, when she became pregnant Telma made it clear that he would have to settle down: 'You'll just have to work as a machinist for the Steiners, Lisette's brother has just left a vacancy.'

'I'd rather die,' Max had thought as he left the house, furious. He was worth more than that.

He had walked around aimlessly with trembling legs. Not daring to go into the shops, he had made do with reading the advertisements pasted to the windows, with apparent nonchalance. At the Gare du Nord he wandered along the platforms. The Orient Express was just about to leave. The sinister grey-green of the metalwork, the dirty curtains at the windows, the screeching from the engines, the pale-faced passengers hurrying to the steps, weighed down by their luggage, running towards a new life and renouncing the old one; that was where it was all happening. How did you get into working on the railways? Max felt inspired by the adventure of it. He could have climbed into a carriage, any one of them. Decided which points to switch for himself.

He knew what lay ahead on his journey only too well. The

rails had been laid down: a straight route with few bends, all the bridges spotted in advance, deserted stations, teeming platforms. What was there to look forward to, and what satisfaction was there to be drawn from watching the predictable countryside unfold? The first stop was Telma. At the second she would have been joined by a couple of children. Where was the element of surprise?

An icy wind swept through the station concourse. The winter sunlight, filtered through the dirty glass roof, threw a gloomy blue veil over the motley crowd of travellers. Max came to a stop in front of the departures board, his face turned up towards it, his hands in his pockets, shivering and indecisive.

'Are you leaving?'

Max jumped in surprise. And there was Henri, staring at him with that lopsided mouth, that half-smile which made him look deceitful. They fell into each other's arms.

'Who knows?' Max replied.

'You must have time for a quick drink?' Henri said appealingly. 'What time's your train?'

Max shrugged his shoulders, smiling, and followed his friend to the station buffet.

With his arms spread out in a crucifix along the back of the seat, his cap all askew and a new suit on his back, Henri had the twinkle in his eye of a boxing manager whose young protégé has just floored a champion.

'You seem to be in good shape,' said Max.

'I won't disguise the fact that things are going better than usual at the moment,' Henri confided.

'And Jacques? Have you had any news from him?'

The three of them had escaped from the work camp together. A good team: Max, who spoke German, was their interpreter; Henri, a former locksmith's apprentice, was the technical expert;

Jacques, a surveyor, was responsible for their travel warrants.

'He took a train last week. He went to Moscow for what they had to offer there. Idealism will get you everywhere.'

As he said this, Henri rolled his eyes, and, without knowing why, Max felt himself falter.

'And so, what good works is the token German doing for the International?'

Max smiled awkwardly. 'I've got married' didn't seem like the best answer, and yet it was the only piece of news that he could give.

'Times are hard,' he said evasively.

'Listen, old man, that's fine. Don't say any more about it. I can read your thoughts. When you've shared "rabbit *à la* fur" with someone, you don't have to explain yourself.'

Three years earlier, half dead with hunger and lost in the middle of the Polish forests, they had managed to catch a rabbit using a snare concocted by Henri. Things had got more complicated when it came to skinning it.

'Chickens are more my department,' Jacques had said, trying to pluck the poor creature.

The other two had laughed, but had not proved any more adept. Eventually, they'd cooked the animal with its skin on, christening the feast with the sweet but not altogether appetising name of 'rabbit *à la* fur'.

'Would you believe,' Henri went on, lowering his voice a little, 'that I'm just about to take over a garage with two mates and we'll be needing someone like you to run it, an upright man I can trust completely.'

'So, you're going over to the other side?' Max asked, relieved, 'You're going to become the boss?'

'Boss? Who said anything about a boss? It's a workers co-operative, old man.'

Henri's face twisted a little further and his fleshy lips drew back to expose two yellowed teeth, horse's teeth that sprouted at random in his otherwise vacant gums. He leant forward and beckoned his friend towards him with his hand. Max didn't like his conspiratorial manner. Something had changed – he wouldn't have been able to say what. Their fraternity had blossomed thanks to the threats they had faced. The links between them had been strengthened by fear and necessity. In a free world, they were no longer the same people. Max could scarcely recognise the man with whom he had shared every meal, next to whom he had spent every night for two months as if, having only ever met him in darkness, he found that he had quite a different face in broad daylight.

'You've got to look after yourself somehow,' Henri spat out quietly, 'because if you let things run their course, the Jews will end up getting everything again.'

He winked and, for a second, Max hesitated before returning the wink. It was a joke, obviously.

Max would have liked to believe that, but he knew. Henri didn't call him the 'token German' for nothing. Max had not revealed anything of his true identity. You couldn't trust anyone. He had often been tempted to confide in his companions, but at the last moment a mysterious force had prevented him. As far as Jacques and Henri were concerned, he was a French soldier of Russian origin who had lived in Germany.

He put his glass down calmly and wiped his lips. Overcome by a sudden urge to strike out, he punched the table and got to his feet without another word.

The next day he had started work as a machinist for the Steiners. No need for any training. He had barely set foot in the workshop before the smell of the fabric, the sheets of newspaper and the tailor's chalk had evoked his father's hunched gestures. He sat himself at a table and set to work, his back very straight.

It was all he asked, not to end up a hunchback by the time he was forty. Apart from that, he didn't really know where he stood any more. Telma didn't ask any questions. She thought that Max had finally accepted his responsibilities and that it made him sad. What could be more normal? Nobody liked saying goodbye to their youth.

Max drummed his fingers on the closed telephone directory, pleased with his list. Five artists was more than enough. He made a note of their telephone numbers in a line down the right-hand side and decided that he had done enough work. Actually, he didn't feel in the least bit tired. It's just that he was hesitating, as he always did at the last minute, before committing the decisive act. If he could have stayed permanently at the frontier of decisions, he would have been perfectly happy. Most men seemed to him to thirst for results, whereas he was happy with prospectives. He felt marginalised by this, as if he were excluded from the pattern that governed the universe.

He was periodically overcome by a surge of shame: he was indecisive and this was a term that implied others that he loathed – timorous, evasive, impotent.

And yet there had been Telma. He had wanted her so badly before the war, this woman married to a local dignitary, this young woman who looked somehow like a widow, who had no children and whose face was closed like a fist. As an inaccessible woman on her husband's arm, she had let her eyes wander surreptitiously towards the boys of her age. If Max had been quicker on the uptake, he would have read the frustration, the appeal and the invitation in the young girl's eyes, but he had been too impressed for that. He had thought that she was way above him, a real lady, and could only read in her expression the superior irony of a woman who can afford to scoff at the innocent.

Why had she chosen him that day, the day that fate took a macabre twist and decided to turn illusion into reality by making her husband disappear into the depths of an oven? Because it was she who came to him when life gradually started up again. On 7th August 1945 she saw him in the street just next to the République and she said, 'We've met.'

Things had happened very quickly. On their third meeting she gave herself to him: slender, golden, with her black dress lifted above her knees to reveal a beauty spot like a clove on her left thigh. Her thin, perfumed shoulders gave themselves up to his kisses, rising and falling to her irregular sighs. Max, in his state of anxiety, interpreted these sighs only as an expression of secret exasperation at his mediocre, inexperienced abilities. She had been married, whereas he could count his conquests on the fingers of one hand. And even then, conquest was a big word; the revolution and then the war had built walls between him and women. Having been a soldier of ideas, he then became a soldier at arms, saving his ardour for his cause and then for combat before watching them expire in the face of flight, famine and the freezing cold.

Telma guided his hands, bashed her knees awkwardly against his, and fretted silently and with her eyes closed. What is she thinking about? he asked himself. A shiver ran down his spine. He was lying on the body of a widow. Perhaps there were still traces in her belly of the dead man, the old man with piercing eyes whose glasses had ended up on the bridge of a German's nose. What better refuge for a man than a woman's vagina? Torn between terror and a desire that had been sharpened by abstinence, he had succumbed. She was already leading the way, passionate, biting and scratching. Such soft skin and such passion. He reassured himself with the thought that she can't have got much out of her marriage.

17

Even after he had married her Max sometimes found himself thinking of the other man and feeling afraid. The dead man was watching them from somewhere.

It was only many years later that he had stopped fearing these ghostly apparitions, the day that Telma had revealed to him one of the keys to her strange past in a moment of confidence that was as rare as it was wonderful. The fat, bearded man had been very erudite, a wise man among wise men who had spent many years studying abroad. He was her mother's much venerated older brother. Max nearly choked.

'You married your uncle!'

'Yup,' Telma replied calmly, 'it was the best thing to do. I hadn't known him as a child. He was much older than my mother. She worshipped him. She spent whole evenings telling us about Jacob, the wise man among wise men. From what she said he was the Messiah in person. Sometimes she cried because he was so far away and she knew he had no family. No wife or children. When he came back I was sixteen. She wanted to give him a present. She gave me.'

Max never knew more than that. Perhaps he would have done better to disguise his astonishment. He had never known how to keep his mouth shut.

'Why did you agree?' What a stupid question! Telma closed in on herself. She had her reasons, in this as in everything.

The memory burned him still, it probably always would. In order to ease the pain, he found himself forced to take action. He would prefer to get involved with his project than to feel the gnawing of regret any longer. His weakness. His over-hasty capitulation. His terribly selfish fear of upsetting her.

He settled himself by the telephone, put his finger on one of the telephone numbers at random and dialled the eight digits that would connect him to. . . . let's see, third name from the top . . . Angus O'Donnell. He closed his eyes and threw himself into the unknown.

'O'Donnell. Hello?'

'Is this Mr Angus O'Donnell?' Max asked.

'Who's calling?'

'My name is Max Opass. I hope I'm not disturbing you.'

'No.'

Then the conversation stopped. Max had no idea what he was going to say to him next.

'Are you a painter?' he asked.

'Yes.'

'I'm ringing you because I would like a portrait.'

'Sorry?'

'Are you a painter, yes or no?'

'Yes.'

'Well then, I'm asking whether you would do a portrait of my wife.'

'A portrait of your wife?'

'That's right,' said Max, opening the first button of his shirt collar.

'I don't do that sort of work,' the painter replied. 'I don't take private commissions.'

Max would have hung up willingly. But it was too late. Once the hook is caught in its head, there's no point in letting the fish go.

'You'll make an exception,' he said. 'I must come and see you.'

'Do you know my work?'

'You are a painter?'

'No, you've misunderstood me. I'm asking why you've called me in particular. How did you get the number?'

'I found it in the phone book.'

'Is this a joke?'

19

'Absolutely not.'

Angus O'Donnell burst out laughing.

'Did you say in the phone book? What an idea! Letting fate dictate its course, in other words. I really like that!'

'So, you will agree to do my wife's portrait?'

'Listen, I've no idea. At the moment I'm working on a fresco for the town of Caen, but . . . come over to my studio, Mr . . .'

'Mr Opass, Max Opass.'

'Yes, come over and see me, we'll talk about this over a drink. Is ten thirty on Wednesday all right for you?'

'Thank you. I'll bring the photos.'

'The photos?'

'The photos of my wife.'

'Bring her with you, it'll be much nicer.'

Nicer wasn't the word, Max thought, but how could he tell him? She can't come because she's dead.

'No, no, it's very kind of you, but I'd prefer to come alone.'

'As you like, Mr Opass, I'll see you on Wednesday.'

Max hung up and wiped his forehead with his handkerchief. He felt very old, almost dead himself. He could always put it off or not go at all. Angus O'Donnell would never be able to get back in touch with him. He was ex-directory. Not so stupid.

Angus

My darling,

Some news from your old father Max.

I hope you won't mind my not waiting for your reply before writing to you again. The old are like children, impatient and capricious. I've had a letter from your brother (the first in six months) and I don't understand a word of it. Perhaps it would be best if I sent you a photocopy of it, but I don't want you to waste any time on my problems. I know you're very busy with your work and the children.

You got on well with him, I think. I only had older sisters. I was the baby of the family. The little afterthought, and the first son. King of the world, in other words. With you two, it was different, there were just the two of you, and your mother was not especially keen to have a boy. Don't tell Lord Byron that, you know how short he is on humour on certain subjects. On the other hand, on some subjects he's got rather too much. He tells me that I'm not old, but that wisdom and childhood come together and 'plough the same river bed', those were his very words. He doesn't say hello or tell me how he is. If it weren't for the envelope I wouldn't have even understood that it was a letter. You know that he writes everything on computer. It's like getting a thingy from the bank. Actually, at one point I think he did mention his new job. A programmer, is that it? I'm not quite sure what that entails. He says: 'in the very entrails of the system, to which I have access, the language I create, thousands of signs? No, from zero all the way to one, a minute infinity, I navigate through, and it's not too badly paid.' It's like a sort of poem, don't you think? It's got a kind of rhythm. Well, I don't know anything about that sort of thing.

At the moment I'm thinking more about painting. I've got a big secret project which I'll tell you about soon. It's very interesting and it makes a change from the bridge. Because, would you believe it, war has been declared at the club. It's Dumas who started it, he just came out and said that we weren't playing 'professionally'. I replied that I didn't know what he'd done before his retirement but that from my point of view being a professional player was not particularly commendable. He got on his high horse about that and I came back at him to say that everyone was entitled to their opinion. The organiser tried to calm him down. They're always afraid one of us is going to have a heart attack. Mrs Brodsky came to find me afterwards to tell me that she didn't think he was very 'sportsmanlike'. She invited me round for tea.

She's propositioned me several times now. I think she's, as you might say, got designs on me. But, well, I've got better things to keep me busy than womanising, as you can well imagine. I haven't been back to the club for a couple of days, I'm waiting for things to settle.

I wouldn't have had time anyway, because I've got all sorts of little problems. Nothing serious, I don't want you worrying, but everything's going wrong. After the watch, it was my car that went and did it. But you couldn't really say I ask too much of it. Two or three outings a week, without getting out of third gear, like with a Rolls-Royce. Yesterday morning I thought I'd really like to go for a walk round Buttes-Chaumont, just to stretch my legs a bit. I go down to the car park, get into the Twingo, turn the key and nothing.

It won't start, it doesn't even make a purr. I take the key out, put it back in again, turn it, nothing. I check that all the lights are switched off. You know, as you get older you tend to lose your mind a bit. 'My old Max,' I said to myself, 'you've gone and left your lights on again.' But no. All present and correct. I open the bonnet and blow on the spark plugs, check the oil level and the water level. It's practically brand new that car, can you believe it?

I go and see the car park attendant and ask him to call for a breakdown truck. You'll never guess what he said. 'I'm sorry, Mr Opass, but you can't get that sort of vehicle down to the third level because of the angle of the access ramp.' So what should I do? He says he hasn't the first idea and that there isn't a sign saying garage above his office. He's young enough to be my son, that chap. No respect. I might as well tell you that this whole episode didn't please me one bit. No breakdown truck is all very well, but how am I to get round it? I'm very happy to go to Buttes-Chaumont on the Metro, and then what?

What really bothered me was that I couldn't understand what the problem was. A car doesn't die just like that, not when it's 18 months old. If your mother had been there, she would have said that it's a sign. 'Everything's going wrong, Max, first the watch, then the car, then us.' She said that sort of thing in the last few days of her life. She said 'The earth is closing back over me,' 'I'm being swallowed up,' and 'The world doesn't want us any more.' I rang the doctor to talk to him about it and he said it was normal, a side-effect of the tranquillisers. Tranquillisers that drive you crazy, what do you think of that? Without going to those sort of extremes, I have to say that this whole business has got me down; I told myself that it would come and get me one morning. What worries me about death is that I'll be there to see it. There'll surely be a moment, a split second, when I realise 'Heck, I'm dying.' Going is fine. The problem is just beforehand.

Each time your mother went out of the house to go to the market it was the same thing: a pain in my stomach, a little sensation of suffocation. Once she was in the stairwell I felt absolutely fine. I even sometimes thought 'Good riddance', but that terrifying little moment . . . I don't know why I'm telling you all this. It's just it wasn't nice having the Twingo dying out of the blue. Mind you, it's been resuscitated now. I really ought to give you the benefit of the happy ending, so to speak. I rang the dealer and said: 'It's Mr Opass calling, my Twingo is kaput, I want a refund.' He sent me a mechanic on foot, as nice as you please. He wasn't much to look at, sort of skew-whiff looking, and then it turns out that he's the Sherlock Holmes of engines. He has a look round the car once, then twice, he opens the bonnet and the boot, and that's the end of the consultation. It was a little light in the boot that had stayed on. He changed my battery and, hey presto, a new car. I gave him a good tip. With all the goings on, I didn't get to Buttes-Chaumont.

I read in the paper that the Tokyo stock-exchange was at an all-time high, please congratulate your husband for me; he may well be a French teacher, but he must be proud of his country. Give the little ones big hugs.

Your old Max who loves you.

'A tie or not a tie, that is the question,' Max said out loud as he contemplated his reflection in the mirror. 'Painters are seriously bohemian.' The tie probably wouldn't be up Angus O'Donnell's street. A scarf would fit the circumstances better. It wasn't a question of competing with the artist by wearing the same para- phernalia, just of choosing an outfit that would be adequate.

Max considered himself an expert in masculine elegance. One of the bitterest battles of his life had consisted in convincing Telma that theory had nothing to do with practice: in other words, even if he was such an expert, he could still quite easily attend the awarding of an Order of Merit in fur boots and could continue to wear a worn-out old scarf stuffed into the collar of his colourless raincoat for dinners in town. 'Once a bumpkin, always a bumpkin,' Telma used to say.

A misunderstood dandy, that's what he had been all his life.

When he arrived at the painter's studio, he thought he would have done just as well to have come with nothing on at all. The frosted glass door, which he had pushed open once he heard the click of the lock, opened into a hall with white walls about four metres high, each one adorned by a canvas with a bright red background on which you could make out a giant, pallid penis, captured in three successive stages of deployment.

'Max!'

Angus had appeared in front of him, his arms spread wide.

'Mr O'Donnell,' Max said shyly as he held his hand out to him.

'Excuse me, I was working,' said the painter to apologize for not coming to greet his guest at the door.

Casting a discreet eye over the paintings around him. Max began to wonder exactly what sort of work he meant.

'Works of youth,' confided the artist.

He must have been in his fifties but appeared younger.

'Right,' the old man said awkwardly.

The studio itself was no more reassuring. A huge room lit by a glass roof at its zenith, with rolls of virgin canvas on the floor. On the walls there were huge sheets of paper held up by black tape and featuring fossilised people, sketches of bodies and faces. A melting of flesh, an air of suffering; all that was missing were the cries. The expressions on the mouths and in the eyes, the grimaces hinted at by the brush strokes, made Max feel uncomfortable.

'Is this your fresco project?' he asked.

'Yes and no. I don't know. I feel a little reluctant to undertake commissions. This excites me and leaves me quite unmoved. A sort of *Guernica* but without the impact, detached from the historical context. Are you interested in painting?'

How could he say no?

'Stupid question,' Angus went on, 'you wouldn't be here. Sit down, please,' said the painter, indicating a sunken leather armchair.

'I came to . . .'

Max was going to talk gibberish, he could tell. He would have preferred to find himself in the middle of the desert without a drop of water.

'How can I explain this to you? Especially if the commission, what was it that you said? If the commission leaves you unmoved. . . .'

'Don't be afraid,' Angus said gently.

He sat down on the floor opposite his new patron, and smiled. He had a good face. A slightly red complexion, thick curly hair, big naive blue eyes and a tiny little mouth that creased maliciously. His hands, which were astonishingly fine with short, chiselled fingers, could easily have belonged to another body. Attached onto the powerful wrists, they looked like the ephemeral replacements for a pair of bear's paws.

'I never invite people to my studio,' he said, coming to the aid of his silent guest. 'I never meet people like you.' The old man shrugged.

'You strike me as quite a character, Max,' went on the painter. 'I shouldn't think your wife has a chance to get bored. It's because of her that you're here isn't it?'

Max blenched. Was Telma getting bored. What a terrible question.

'I love faces,' Angus said without waiting for a reply. 'Human faces. The whole body is contained in the face, like a small-scale map. They talk about figurative art. But what could possibly be more abstract than a face? The skin is just a tissue of thoughts.'

What a magnificent voice he had! Gentle, soothing, with barely a hint of an accent. Max listened to him, smiling. His nerves gradually dissolved, giving way to the charm of finding himself in totally alien surroundings. He didn't understand everything but let himself be lulled, as if by the fitful chugging of a train. With each sentence a new landscape sketched itself in his mind's eye, tall grasses, fragile poppies, carved dunes, rounded dunes, the sunlit slopes of a mountain top, the dark disturbing depths of a lake.

The rising sun lit the room, and this tide of light swept away all traces of anxiety. Max felt his heart shaking itself free, shedding the weight of several decades and rediscovering the feeling of eternal calm experienced by the little boy crouching in his mother's farmyard. Wearing just his underpants in high summer, he would hold out his hands to the boldest chicks and felt he had been adopted into the uncomplicated world of the poultry. With the August sunlight warming his back, he would chirrup happily and, drowned in the present, savour each crumb of happiness, the brightness of the scarce blades of grass, the glistening pebbles, all things for which he didn't even have a name yet.

'I wanted to create a layered effect with the composition,' Angus continued, indicating the fresco with a large, sweeping movement of his hand. 'Can you see how the bodies fit together without crushing each other, cover each other without being weighed down, a sort of sexual prehistory where there is no tension, just contact, juxtaposition.'

From where he was in the armchair, Max let his eye wander over the walls which suddenly came to life when a door that he had not noticed, a white door barely distinguishable from the white of the walls, opened.

'Diane, my love,' said Angus without looking at the woman who had come in. 'This is Max. Max . . . what was it again?'

Max said nothing. If he really had forgotten his own surname he would not have been more silent. The woman who had just come in had no face. Her eroded nose barely stood out from her other features, her colourless lips could only be distinguished by their very slight swelling, the absence of eyebrows made her eyes seem enormous, as if they had no lids; as for the ears, Max would not have been able to say, because her head was covered by a brightly coloured scarf, knotted in a turban.

'My husband likes surprises,' she said, and Max thought he saw her smile.

How long had she burned for? How many days had passed until the pain was forgotten? And her body, what state was her body in?

'Opass, Max Opass, it's come back to me now,' Angus said as he made his way over to his wife and took her in his arms.

Max rose to his feet, as stiff as if he had risen from his own grave.

'My respects, Mrs O'Donnell,' he said, holding out his hand to her.

Diane's palm was as soft as a child's.

I mustn't ask any questions, Max told himself, I must behave as if there is nothing unusual. He suddenly thought that he would never have the courage to tell Angus that Telma was no longer of this world. Some misunderstandings are more difficult to unravel than the most violent attachments.

Diane asked them whether they would like some tea or coffee. Max, who was jittering and trembling imperceptibly, had completely turned to ice.

'A cup of tea, if it's no trouble,' he said looking in her direction without actually focusing on her face.

'Yes, a cup of tea,' said Angus, 'now, that's a good idea. We always drink coffee, too much coffee.'

The painter had lost some of his self-assurance. When Diane had left the room, he came over to Max and, taking him by the shoulder, started pacing around the room as if it were a garden. Please don't let him say anything, thought Max, don't let him tell me about his devastating life, how he met the most beautiful woman in the world, how they had a crash in a propeller plane in which they lost – who knows? – two of their children. Make him go on talking about dead leaves and prehistoric sexuality, harmless things that don't mean anything.

Max was terribly afraid of other people's unhappiness. His panic usually translated itself into the sudden paralysing of some of his joints. Just one glance at the horrors of life turned him to stone. He had had his fair share of suffering, though. Orphaned by his mother at three, he had watched his little neighbour die in just two days from some infection in her chest, and years later several of his fellow soldiers had been hacked to pieces before his very eyes, many of his friends and almost all of his family had been turned into bars of soap in the camps, but he had always bounced back, courageous and happy that, at the end of the day, he had been spared by fate. He couldn't help thinking

that every time death made another strike amongst his entourage
it was saying 'Damn, missed again!' as it watched him get back
to his feet and make a run for it. There had been that first tear
for Telma, but wasn't it the advent of his own end that made
him sad? I'm appallingly selfish, he thought. To his great surprise,
he had no feelings of guilt about it. He just didn't want to have
anything to do with unhappiness, that was all.

'The idea came to me when I was writing a paper about the
Umbrian School,' said Angus. 'I've always had a tremendously
soft spot for those predictable compositions, those coded looks.
The hands and the feet most frequently elude current aesthetic
conventions, you could say it's the artist's signature. I did some
valuation work a few years ago for a dairy products company.
You take what work you can. But I'm boring you with my stories,
kitchen sink and all.'

'On the contrary,' said Max far too enthusiastically.

He was quite happy to go on hearing about that particular
kitchen. So long as it had nothing to do with injuries and acci-
dents. Be that as it may, he didn't have any choice; if he left the
studio after what he had seen it would be as good as saying 'I'm
sorry, Mr O'Donnell, but your wife's burns are really not very
appetising and I'd rather go somewhere else.' He would, therefore,
have to put a brave face on it, get out the photographs, remain
evasive on the subject of Telma – he would just have to pretend
that she was very shy – and pay the bill.

As he spoke, Angus guided his guest in eccentric circles round
the workshop. They stopped next to one wall, and the painter
started stroking his sketch with the tips of his fingers.

'So I started with the hands and the feet. I waited on it hand
and foot, you might say.'

He burst out laughing and Max copied him.

'Hands reaching out, feet leaving the ground, neither coming together nor tangling with each other, something very fluid, rounded even ... have you ever attended a spiritual seance?'

Without waiting for Max's reply he went on:

'I did it for several years. Don't worry, I can assure you that I don't believe in all that twaddle.'

Reassured, Max was not. He felt out of place and inappropriate, like a chicken in front of a pebble.

'What interested me was the contact from one hand to another, all that energy passing just from one finger to the next. It was also really beautiful to watch that great flower evolving over the table, like a giant sunflower, a wonderful decapitated heart.'

A decapitated heart, Max repeated in his head. Whatever next.

'We did it at nightfall, in the half-dark, by the light of a candle. I learned more about chiaroscuro in those seances than in five years at the Beaux-Arts. What I've tried to convey, what I'm trying to get across in this fresco is the way that a touch looks at us. Do you see what I mean?'

Max bent his head to one side. His host was on a roll. Max had quickly grasped the fact that he didn't need to give him any encouragement for him to continue.

'Are you familiar with Braille? I've studied it in detail. When Diane had trouble with her eyesight, we worked on it together.'

Don't let her be blind on top of everything else, Max prayed just in case.

'The operation was miraculous and Diane gave up on it, but I discovered some incredible things. The pads of my fingers became as sensitive as they must have been when I was still a baby. You can't imagine what a relief it is for a painter to close his eyes. No longer representing what you see, freeing yourself from sight, from your own sight, in order to free yourself completely from the looks of other people. Do you follow me?'

Following him was saying a lot, but Max was beginning to get caught up in the game. In his own way, he knew quite a bit about hands, and their intelligence.

One night, somewhere in Poland, his fingers had begun to freeze. First he had felt the cold, then pain, terrible pain, and when the pain had suddenly stopped, it gave way to fear. He had brought his bandaged middle finger to his lips, but the finger had remained inert, with less feeling in it than a twig. This once supple and agile snake which had a sort of independent life was very nearly lost to him. Just a few more moments and the fingers would have come away from the palm, like so many stalactites.

He was alone in the woods. His heart had started beating far too quickly. If he had listened to his mind he would have set off through the woods, running dead ahead and yelling. But his hands, his incredibly cunning hands, had used what little life was left in them to tell him what to do. With the help of his teeth, he had torn off the strips of cloth that were bound round his hands as gloves and had thrown himself to the ground, burying his arms in the snow. He didn't know what he was doing. Terrified by the thought that the slightest movement might tear his fingers off, he stayed motionless. He concentrated on the rare noises in the forest, the cracking of a trunk, the whistling of the wind, a block of snow detaching itself from a branch and collapsing in a muffled crash.

A hooting sound arose from nowhere, unreal. An owl. The owl that lived under the roof in the barn at his grandmother's house when he was still a little boy who would fall asleep as he milked the cows with his head resting on the animal's warm flank. Hoo-hoo, hoo-hooo! he called, and the owl replied. There was probably a barn very nearby, hidden in the dark woods, or perhaps a hut, a door, a roof, four walls. Oh, to huddle up in there and to shut out the blizzard that was devouring his hands. He had made himself a muff of snow using his knees, his chin and his cheeks. His body no longer knew its head from its tail. Then he got to his feet with his arms held tightly to his chest, and he started to walk, slowly, with his ears on the alert. His eyes couldn't see anything that looked in the least like a house but his hearing guided him through the brambles, into the dells, over the fallen branches.

He almost crashed into the door. With a lunge of his shoulder he launched himself inside. A tiny ray of moonlight streamed in through the skylight in the roof, and for an instant it was reflected in the golden eye of the owl perched on the beam, a stocky little mantle clock in feathers with its round head barely tilted to one side. He shut the latch and crumpled onto the frozen ground, lulled by the maternal hooting of the great calm bird. Little by little, warmed by his breath, the muff of snow had melted. When his thumb, the first to revive, had made its presence known, he was bowled over as he never had been before and as he would be only twice more, on the 9th of July 1946 and the 4th of March 1948, the moment that each of his new-born children had first squeezed the index finger that he held out to them.

'*Tea is served*,' said Diane, putting a tray down on the floor in the middle of the room.

'Those are the only words of English that my stupid wife has managed to learn after twenty years of living together,' Angus said tenderly.

'It's not a bad start,' the old man said clumsily.

'What a sense of humour, Max, what a sense of humour! Black humour, like my own. You need it, I can assure you, to live with a ghost like this,' Angus said, stroking the nape of his wife's neck.

To Max's great surprise, Diane pulled a face. She suddenly looked like one of those Chinese masks that had frightened Nadya and Basile so much when they had visited the Museum of Popular Arts and Traditions when they were little.

In this tortured state, Diane's face came to life and, when she started laughing, Max was amazed to find that he was somehow titillated.

'We're weird, aren't we?' said Angus.

Max couldn't help himself smiling. His own wife had burned down to ashes. Gruesome analogy.

'When you get to eighty,' he replied, 'you've seen a thing or two, you know. You don't ask so many questions any more.'

'Because you know that the answers will always be disappointing?' asked Diane.

'I'm not a philosopher, my dear,' Max replied, terrified by the turn that the conversation was taking.

He was uncomfortable as soon as he had to put his thoughts into words. He was constantly assailed with impressions and ideas, but he refused to organise them. He was even careful to silence his slightest intuitions, for fear of being taken for a 'stupid old fool', a label that he had, happily, never had pinned on him. He had seen so many of those ageing fathers who endlessly trot out their theories and their beliefs, congratulating themselves all day for the wisdom that time and experience have allowed them to accumulate. He had seen their sons' hatred and their daughters' disappointment. The brand of wisdom which he himself had built up as time went by was, in a nutshell, his selfishness, and it had been his saving grace. *Let them do as they see fit so long as I can carry on doing as I please.*

'I left school at thirteen,' Max announced.

He let himself fall back into the only armchair in the studio, exhausted by so much truthfulness. A second earlier he would not have been able to predict what he was going to say and yet that simple sentence said everything. His robustness, his shame, his glory, his uncertainty and practically fifty years of conflict with the intellectual, well brought-up Telma, Telma who saw herself as a younger sister of Elsa Triolet's because she had read everything and could explain photosynthesis to their dumbstruck children.

'If you know so much, my dear,' Max had said to her one acrimonious morning, 'why do you work as a finisher for the Steiners? Why didn't the Sorbonne come to find you?'

'Do you really want an answer to that? Perhaps you want me to refresh your memory? Does the war mean anything to you?'

'Very vaguely. But what I remember very clearly is your wonderful husband. What was his name again? The old man who took you out for walks on Saturdays with his goatee beard, his walking stick and his pretty little slip of a girl. You were already not so clever then.'

It was a paltry victory. How could he feel that he had gained anything from it? As soon as she stumbled, Telma took him with her into a great chasm of bitterness. He didn't feel strong enough to give her back the dashed hopes of the young girl she had once been. When he had met her, there was nothing left to mend, she was like a clock without a pendulum, but it was closed, so tightly closed, that before finding the reason, before understanding why the hands no longer swept round the face, you could wear yourself out checking the dozens of springs and cogs. Right from the beginning he had sensed that her heart had somehow broken down, that there was no tick and no tock. What could he do about it? He hadn't been to university. He was good with his hands. Yes, that was it. That was all. And on the rare occasions when he succeeded in soliciting a smile, a sigh or a cry, it had been like that that he had done it, with the tips of his fingers, skin against skin, slow manual work, far less gratifying than you would think. Reading poems and pretty words that women like was too much for him.

'Did you bring the photos?'

'The photos,' Max repeated absentmindedly.

'Max's wife is invisible,' Angus told Diane. 'He wants me to paint her portrait from photographs. What do you think of that?'

'I didn't know you did portraits,' she said sadly. 'It was bound to happen. If you want my advice, you'd do well to start by doing yourself. Portrait of the artist as a beautiful greying fifty-something. It wouldn't bring in as much as the painter laureate of the town of Caen but it would at least have the merit of being courageous.'

Max looked at her with no apprehension this time. He knew this piece of music . . . these women, all the same! Burnt or not burnt, dead or alive, hands on sabres and I'll get on and lop off your arms, your throat, the lot. She had her fair share to say and to get off her chest, too. Mind you, she should have considered herself lucky to have found a lover with a face on her like that!

How could he conceive such thoughts? Especially when you really looked at it, that smooth skin, an impassive mask pierced by two sparkling eyes under the multicoloured turban, and the body – a dancer's body, perhaps – with a very straight back, knees turned out, and high, firm breasts. An elf who would never have bags under her eyes or creases at the corners of her lips.

'Don't worry, Diane,' he said with an unexpectedly authorita-tive tone. 'It's not what you think. It's a very special case. An exceptional case. Angus won't do any other portraits. He can't stand them, anyway. He told me. I can assure you. It's a special situation. What he's trying to get across without shocking you – he's going about it quite cleverly, mind you, "invisible" was a good choice of word – is that my wife is dead.'

There was a long silence. Diane poured the tea. Angus knelt next to her. Max drummed the armrest of his chair, not displeased with the little effect he had had. Then he took out the five photographs that he had chosen and which, he thought, would be the only clues surrendered to the artist for him to complete this work of desecration.

Virginie

Max was standing in the kitchen sprinkling sliced shallots over his piece of hake. 'A pinch of salt, a pinch of pepper, and bingo! close up the papillote.' He realised that he was talking to himself but he had decided to allow himself to do this in two sets of circumstances: preparing meals and DIY. Every time he positioned a nail he allowed himself a running commentary of the situation: 'I'm going to have to find a solution. If I put it too high up I'm going to have trouble with the cupboard; if I put it too low, it'll be trailing in the sink.'

It wasn't a question of cheating loneliness – Max had never suffered from that evil – rather of commentating on the action in order to give it more weight, and to ensure that nothing had been forgotten. When he had started cooking two years previously, he had had one or two very unfortunate experiences. Telma, who was bedridden, could have advised him but he had his pride and he didn't want to tire her at any cost. You only needed to concentrate on the end result to deduce the series of ingredients and procedures required. At that time, quite a few pans of meatballs and a good many cakes had ended up in the bin. Max had not been discouraged. Thanks to the power of speech, his previously unexploited culinary talents had been revealed. By virtue of his patience and his oral hummings and hawings, he had become quite a respectable cake-maker.

The day Telma tasted his lemon meringue pie she pushed the plate away after two mouthfuls. 'Don't you like it?' Max had asked slyly. 'It's too sweet,' she lied. In fact she was piqued that she was no longer the only master on board. 'He's chivvied me out of my kitchen, soon he'll be chivvying me out of this bed,' she thought. Max could have reproached himself for aggravating his wife's condition when she was suffering enough already, but he wasn't eating from that particular loaf. When she stopped breathing a few months later he felt unmitigated sadness: he had had nothing to do with it, Telma had died of her multifarious illnesses.

'A drizzle of olive oil when it comes out of the oven, a few drops of lemon juice, and there we are, it's ready.' Accompanied by a slice of toast covered with chopped white onions, this was a feast fit for a king. While he was enjoying his meal he set about imagining the afternoon's rendezvous. It was a woman this time. He hoped she would be young and pretty, why deny himself these pleasures? He was in the mood for turning on the charm. His visit to Angus had taught him a lot and, determined to pass himself off as a connoisseur, he practised a few key words: 'Play of light, composition. The whole body is in the face,' he declaimed in a resonant voice. Half past one, it was time to go.

He wasn't what one would call a woman-chaser; on reflection, he was even quite the opposite: women chased after him. Since his childhood he had been accustomed to spending a lot of time in the company of women, and he knew how to be sufficiently discreet and attentive to earn their kindly approval. He didn't make any particular effort, their hearts just fell at his feet like poppy petals before he had even tried to pick them. A salesgirl on the toy counter at the Galeries Lafayette had asked him to marry her while he was trying to extract information about electric trains. The woman at the dry cleaners in the rue de Lancry had let him know that it would be 'whenever he wanted'. Even the headmistress at Nadya's school had made eyes at him as she told him yet again that he had a Slav soul that she found absolutely irresistible.

That was a long time ago, when he was still trying to provoke Telma's jealousy. She herself didn't leave people indifferent. Between 30 and 45 she had done nothing but grow more beautiful. She knew it and derived some pleasure from the fact, especially when she went into a shop with her daughter and they were taken for sisters. It was a polite little lie in which she delighted, and Nadya was so good and gentle that she didn't even have the poor taste to take offence at it.

Her silhouette had not changed; she was all leg, a bit flat-chested, with beautiful shoulders and a supple waist. Her face, which was often inert, frozen in some mysterious hesitation, had taken a good long time to produce its first wrinkle. A real beauty. But there were no hearts lying at her feet. She could turn you to ice with one glance, and Max sometimes had to remind himself that she was his wife before mustering the courage to approach her.

She was probably faithful to me. That's quite something after forty-nine years. Not even a tiny kiss on the corner of the lips from some passing stranger or some old friend making a late declaration? Not one inappropriate – but oh! so delicious – gesture from an inspired young man risking it all to have it all?

As if she were not made of flesh and blood. Except. Max had been known to dream of her in another man's arms. Probably to give himself greater freedom with the wanderings which he allowed himself. One morning, when the children had gone to school and he had dropped Telma at the Steiners, he had stopped at a café terrace on the Grands Boulevards. He had taken the morning off to pick up the children's birth certificates because they were going off on a school trip with their Russian master. Sitting in the sun, delicately stirring his spoon round in his cup, he had felt completely drained.

Nearly twenty years of marriage and, just like that, step by step, hand in hand, they would follow their straight and narrow path, guiding each other to the edge of the world, to the end of time. Polite to the very last: 'Take my hand, step into the ferry, we just have to cross the river and we'll see each other on the other side.' 'No, you go first, please.' An eternal love, for life, till death.

In a fit of rebellion, he had made a pass at the woman at the next table. An illusory escape. At the end of the morning, the passports still hadn't been done and Max's heart was corroded by his betrayal.

'Virginie! I hope you don't mind my calling you Virginie; you could be my daughter.'

'Come in, Mr Opass.'

The young woman didn't look as if she felt quite right and Max was somewhat thrown.

'I'm not disturbing you, am I? We did say two o'clock?'

'Yes. No. Well, I mean no, yes. You're not disturbing me and we did say two o'clock. Let me take your coat.'

She was in her forties, with a lovely face and a hesitant voice that was somehow muted. The other type. Yes, that's right, there were two types of women, those who are full of resentment and those who are full of pain. Virginie clearly belonged to the second category.

Max went into the sitting-room, a dark cluttered room. There was a tricycle with its front wheel and half of the handlebar stuck in a Greek urn, a television precariously balanced on a pile of old newspapers, a lamp without a shade on a round table that was laden with books and covered in a constellation of biscuit crumbs. It smelt of bleach. Max melted indulgently when Virginie said:

'Don't look at the mess, please, what with the children, the cat and . . . well . . .'

She ran her hand through her hair, revealing a pretty forehead that was perfectly smooth except for a single line at the root of the nose.

'Quite,' said Max who could sense that she was at breaking point. 'Children make a lot of mess. Don't you have a studio?'

Virginie gave a half-hearted smile and said nothing. She was waiting for a studio to fall out of the sky. She couldn't say, 'No, I paint in the kitchen.' She didn't want to talk about that.

'Do sit down,' she said to Max, indicating a sofa that was so low that the old man felt as if he were falling into space before he collapsed into the sagging cushions.

I'll never get back up, he thought. Virginie Lazieu sat down opposite him, bolt upright on a slightly crooked cane chair.

'Is it for a portrait?' she asked.

The little poster from which Max had taken notes in the art shop next to the grocer had filled him with enthusiasm: 'Artist will carry out all your wishes.' He had given up on the telephone directory in order to throw himself into the adventure of the small ads. Some people used the same methods to find a new wife. With him it was different. He was looking for a wife, not a new one, a wife who had been his for fifty years.

'That's right,' said Max. 'You're a different kind of painter. I mean, with you it's not blah-blah-blah. With you it's straight to the point. Well, I say that because I've met one . . . I've got a friend who's a painter and, you've no idea, he never stops talking. When I go round to his studio, I get the whole guided tour. I've learnt more about the play of light having a cup of coffee with him . . . so, there we are, I am here for a portrait of my late wife.'

'Yes?'

Virginie was listening quietly, her lips quivering, her right

47

cheek contracted by some nervous tic. She had her hands on her knees and Max couldn't help noticing that there wasn't a trace of paint on them; the nails had been bitten down till they bled.

'My wife left me a year ago and I've found it difficult getting back on my feet since then,' he said.

God, it was easy speaking to this little poppet. She was nice and quiet and didn't interrupt.

'We'd been married for fifty years. Forty-nine to be precise. But, what difference does it make?'

'None at all,' Virginie replied firmly.

'Well said, little one. It doesn't make any difference. You get used to each other, you get to know each other, that's what everyone thinks, anyway. In fact,' Max hesitated a moment, asking himself whether Virginie would follow him as meekly over this territory as the rest. 'In fact, it's not like that. You never get used to someone and you don't know them any more after fifty years than on the first day.'

He started to laugh and Virginie did the same.

'You understand what I'm saying, I think. You know, some mornings you ask yourself that extraordinary question: "But who is this person sleeping in my bed?"'

'Who is this person?' Virginie repeated, looking thoughtful. 'I don't know. For a long time, I believed that it was myself.'

She stopped speaking and stared at a point above Max's head and slightly to the right. A charming confidante, no doubt a capable artist but sensitive too. From the minute he set foot in her home, he had measured the distance between this painter and the one he had met a week earlier. This was a long way from the ramblings about figurative concepts and a fresco of piles of autumn leaves, this was in the very concrete world of children and home. They wouldn't discuss the price for long here, it would be reasonable and moderate, like everything else.

48

Max preferred not to think of the fee that Angus would ask of him. He had read in the paper that some contemporary painters, of which he himself had never heard, even those who were not in great demand, asked as much as thirty thousand francs for a little painting thirty centimetres square. Thirty thousand, that was quite something; but he had made a point of telling Angus that he wanted something discreet, twenty-five by fifteen. Would that put it at twenty five thousand or at fifteen thousand? It was probably negotiable. Mind you, even at fifteen thousand . . .

'I would sometimes wake up in the middle of the night,' Virginie went on, 'and I would comfort myself with the thought that it was me, the shape next to me. You know the story of Goldilocks? "Who's been sleeping in my little bed?" Actually, I never got used to having someone between my sheets. It's too much of an invasion. And someone in my space. After a while, I even felt I had someone inside my head. I was married for ten years.'

She smiled without focusing her eyes. Max didn't understand much about modern love.

'It's a lottery. You never know who you'll end up with, do you?' he said. 'I've brought you a few photographs.'

He took a box out of his jacket pocket.

'They are slides that I've had made from the originals. It cost me a small fortune this business but, well, you do have to make a few sacrifices.'

Virginie held out her hand. She carefully lifted off the plastic lid and took out the five pictures. One by one she paraded them past her eyes. She was turned towards the window, screwing up her eyes.

'Can you see them?' Max asked. 'They're a bit small, but I thought that with a projector . . . do you have a slide projector?'

Virginie said yes. It was very good news. Max, feeling a surge of optimism, wanted to get up and look at the tiny reproductions. He pushed up with his hands and leant forwards, in the hopes of swinging his centre of gravity upwards. In vain. His backside rose a few centimetres only to settle again even more deeply into the trap of the sunken sofa. He sighed, resigned to waiting, immobile, while Virginie completed her scrutiny.

The body is a prison, thought Max; you've barely learnt to master the most simple gestures before you start to be trapped by it. Every year, every day and, in the end, every hour puts a new brick in the wall of the enclosure. It was a good twenty years since he had run, and how many decades had gone by since he last jumped? He was the mason, the guard and the prisoner all at once. Only death would deliver him. But what hope was there for a life without the body? It struck him that his soul would never have the strength to lift itself; and as for his mind, its terrifying dissolution had already begun. His memory was still there. A frail ladder of rope with which to climb back through time. In his memories, Max saw himself leaping like a young goat. What use could there be for this strange tool? It was in this unanswerable question that he was most clearly aware of the presence of God. It must have taken more than just an amoeba to invent memory.

Max looked at his watch and wondered whether he would have time to go and play a game of bridge before the club closed. He felt tired and no longer had the strength to play the lady-killer. He might as well be lucid on this: nothing more could happen to him. The next major event in his life he knew only too well. Some surprise! Yet he still found the strength to get up in the mornings and he still nourished some small hopes, rather like a ruined circus manager who recycles his career into trading performing fleas.

What a grotesque situation! It pained him to think about it.

He felt as if he were waking from the dreams of a young man
who had fallen asleep fifty years earlier, a dream of a life that
was as brief as a single night. But he didn't have the right words
at his disposal to give shape to this strange impression that swept
over him. He thought of the plastic bags that are heaved back
and forth by the waves and the tide, and that you sometimes
find, billowing with air, like sickly bubbles of foam on the surface
of the water. These indestructible bags go on long journeys that
hold no great interest. Humans pay a small fortune to tread the
same path, to what end? He too had travelled a great deal, he
had moved in time and space and, all along the way, his only
obsession had been to resist, to remain intact, from one end of
the earth to the other, over rivers and seas, to end up here.

'What was your wife's name?' Virginie asked as she put the
slides away.

'Telma,' Max said in a troubled voice.

It was so strange saying that name. A call that would never
again receive a reply. One of the terribly fragile exhibits in the
museum of his memory. A secret crypt into which no one would
ever go.

'She was called Telma,' he repeated.

'That's a brand of soups, isn't it? Jewish soups, I think.'

'They're called "kosher", actually.'

'Kosher soups, then. I remember because when I was pregnant
with Paulo I thought I was carrying a girl, and one day in Mono-
prix I went past the shelves with all the Jewish things . . . I mean
the kosher things; I saw the chicken noodle soup with the name
Telma on it and I thought it would be a pretty name for my
baby.'

'Isn't Paulo the name of a mint?'

'It's not written the same way. The sweet is P-o-l-o.'

Max went for a mental wander round the hypermarket of

humanity. In the Jewish department they'd run out of stock of little children born near Warsaw between 1930 and 1940.

'Do you think you'll be able to do it?' he asked.

'That I'll be able to do what?' asked Virginie.

'The portrait. Do you have time? Do you think it will be easy?'

Virginie put the slides down and, looking up at the ceiling, ran her hand slowly through her hair.

'Yes, I certainly think so. Time ... I've got nothing but time. Easy, that's saying a lot.'

What sort of mind did this young woman have? She listened attentively with her eyebrows knitted and her mouth slightly pinched. Her eyes would suddenly freeze, on the lookout for something. She seemed ready to solve the most scabrous equations. And to each question she gave an answer, perfectly in order, as if she were numbering them.

'What did you do before you became a painter?' asked Max, party to an inexplicable intuition.

'I was a switchboard operator,' replied Virginie.

She blushed as soon as she had said it, knowing that she had surrendered herself and discredited herself in one go. A really disappointing victim for an expert torturer, thought Max. A little queen of connections; it didn't take much to make her talk.

'But I've always loved painting,' she added quickly, hoping to salvage something.

'I'm not asking you to be Renoir,' said Max 'and certainly not Picasso. So, switchboard operator or not, it doesn't matter a jot to me. I don't have any prejudices, you know. Take my wife, for example, she worked all her life in the rag trade when she could have been a university professor. She really had a head of gold, as my people say. An extremely brilliant woman, I promise you, and that didn't stop her spending her life plying a needle. But without shame. There's no shame in doing a manual job, is there?

I myself have retired from working in clothing and that doesn't mean that I don't know anything about anything. I take interest in things, I gather information about them. I don't do the rounds of the museums, it's true, but that's because my feet hurt. Who knows what I might have been if I'd had the choice?'

'I've always wanted to be a painter,' she said, 'but I left home too soon. My parents didn't want to give me any money because I was on drugs. I wasn't really on drugs at all, of course.'

'Of course,' Max repeated, to convince himself.

A mother. Little children, the upside down tricycle. Drugs, what a nightmare!

'As a girl, I was a bit too free and easy for their liking. I liked going to parties, dancing, meeting boys, but I liked work too. At the time I think I liked everything in life. Nothing passed me by.'

Virginie gathered up a few crumbs on the table top. She pushed them into a line; a square shape and then a triangle appeared. She scattered them again, sighing loudly, and went on.

'I was very affected by a philosophy lesson about time in the sixth form. I couldn't possibly regurgitate it word for word, but what I remember was the link between time and space. Mme Hazée, the teacher, explained that the passage of time only becomes apparent to us in relation to space. That's not very clear, I don't think.'

She lowered her eyes and bit her lip.

'On the contrary,' said Max. 'For someone like me who's never had the opportunity to study philosophy, it's very interesting. Go on, Virginie, please.'

'It was to do with the distance travelled or not travelled in a given time. At one point it became more complicated and I'm not sure that I understood what Mme Hazée was trying to tell us. But it's stayed with me, embedded here –' she lifted her fringe and clapped her hand on her forehead '– like a nail. I will try to explain it to you. You'll indulge me, won't you?'

'Without boasting,' said Max, 'I can assure you that you'd have trouble finding a better audience than me.'

Virginie smiled, balled her hands into tight fists and embarked.

'As time goes by, space becomes smaller . . . Yes, that's it. But the opposite is also true. As time goes by, space becomes bigger. At each stage, there is a crossroads. You choose a path, and this choice cancels all the other options out. You can't go backwards. If you're right-handed, you will never be left-handed. Do you see what I mean?'

Max nodded.

'As time goes by, you make more and more choices, and the space left to you becomes smaller and smaller. As time goes by, the space between us and our dreams gets wider and wider. I will never be a great painter.'

Virginie stopped speaking for a moment, gathered up the crumbs with one hand, slid them into the crook of her palm and threw them into a flower pot.

'I had to earn a living somehow, so I applied for a job as a switchboard operator in a big hotel. You might not think so, but it's quite a responsibility. When I met my husband, I thought things would change. He was older than me, a wine merchant. I met him at the hotel. He was quite cultured; it was he who gave me my first set of oils. But oil paints are very difficult to work. I settled for acrylics, do you know them?'

'Acrylics, you say?'

Max remembered the invasion of Nylon, that revolutionary fabric that didn't crease and dried in an afternoon. Telma had been suspicious of it. 'With silk, you know where it comes from,' she had said. 'It's natural. I can't see myself wearing petrol on my back. It's disgusting.'

'So you find worm's spit more attractive, do you?' Max had replied. Why was it that he always had to feel like a beggar compared to her, a sort of hearty peasant who was a bit rough round the edges?

'They're really beautiful. They give bright, really striking colours,' said Virginie. 'And it washes off in water. You could say that was a minor detail but, what with the children, I spend my life doing the washing. I've stopped working. It was probably a mistake. One of the few paths left open to me, and I abandoned it. My husband didn't get on very well with me. I let him down. When the children were born, I didn't want anything any more. Even painting seemed superfluous. I liked looking after them, that was all I needed to fill my days. My husband liked going out, travelling. I was pretty and I think that flattered him. But I no longer felt like dressing up. As soon as we left the house, I felt as if I had abandoned the children. He couldn't stand it. He left. I've been putting ads in the shops round here for a week. I don't know if it'll come to anything, but I think it's still the best thing I can do to buy some time.'

She stopped talking and looked at Max inquisitively. She was asking his opinion and it would probably have been easy to reassure her, but the old man was somewhere else, lost among the many crossroads that he had come to himself.

'If you like, I can show you what I do,' she suggested, getting to her feet. 'Don't move. I'll bring my portfolio in here.'

She left the room. Max watched her go. She had a jerky way of walking. In the corridor, when she probably thought she couldn't be seen, she pulled her sweater down and turned her skirt round so that the zip was in the right place. Funny creature, thought Max. He was fascinated by these apparently meaningless little gestures. Telma didn't have any little habits like that, those constant coquettish touches. She didn't look at herself much in mirrors, and she brushed her hair once in the morning and once in the evening. And yet, she was impeccably turned out all through the day. He would have liked to have known her as a little girl, to have seen her playing tag or hide-and-seek, to have caught her as she pulled straw from her brown curls, to have heard her catching her breath with red cheeks and sweat glowing on her forehead. Why did she have to be so serious?

There was only one summer when he thought he had seen signs of the delightful little demon in her. It was hardly anything. A new gesture. A hand movement that she suddenly invented at thirty-five. Had she seen it in a film? That didn't seem likely. Her intention was more meaningful than that. Two or three times a day she would stare into space and lift her right arm to put a lock of hair back in place, always the same one, a sort of kiss curl which lolled over her eyebrow.

They had been invited to spend a week in the Steiners' holiday house. Max was not enthusiastic. Why would people like that invite their workers? 'Dora and I were friends before, in Russia, when my father was the mayor in our village. We went to school together. I lent her my dolls. Her mother was dead and I . . .'

'You felt sorry for the little orphan just as she now feels sorry for her little seamstress.'

'That's got nothing to do with it. And, anyway, it's an opportunity for the children to go to the country. We might even get as far as the coast.' The decision was taken.

'What sweet children you have! Let me help you, do call me Victor. Dora has stayed at the house to get your rooms ready.'

It was the only car parked in front of the station, a pre-war model – his holiday car, Max thought. Victor opened the door for Telma and held out his hand to help her climb into the car. 'My dear friend,' Max kept saying to himself during the journey. On the terrace after dinner I will call him 'my dear friend'. The rest will come of its own accord; there's no need to premeditate about it too much. He had turned to look at his boss for a moment before facing the evidence: there would never be any 'dear friend' between them. Victor Steiner was grimacing slightly, sitting bolt upright with his hands clamped to the steering wheel and screwing up his eyes. Whatever the situation, he always looked like that, like someone who has trouble swallowing.

The children, who hadn't stopped running up and down in the train, had gone to sleep in their mother's arms. A few minutes before they arrived, Max turned to Telma. She didn't notice straight away that he was looking at her. With her eyes fixed on the middle of the windscreen, she lifted her right arm and put the curl back in place. In the summer light her minute pupils made her eyes look lighter, the brown of her irises turned to gold. She suddenly realised she was being watched and she let her arm drop down onto her daughter's shoulder.

'There,' said Virginie, putting a big portfolio down on the table, 'that'll give you an idea.'

Max smiled at her, slightly lost.

'There's a bit of everything. I haven't put them in any order. I'd like to do an exhibition, but I don't know where. I'll leave you to look at them.'

She opened the portfolio and took a few sheets of paper from it.

The moment of truth, Max thought. He was going to have to get up. He could always ask her for help. There was no shame in it for an old man like him. Gathering his strength, he put his closed fists on either side of his body, took a deep breath and closed his eyes, concentrating just as hard as a rocket pilot in the moment of take-off – at least, that was how he imagined the scene. Virginie was watching him without grasping the tragic or

– depending on how you looked at it – comic aspect of the situation. She was impatient, rather excited; it wasn't often that she had the opportunity to show off her work, and even less common for her to receive a client. At the end of the secret countdown, the miracle happened and Max got to his feet, with his nose in the air and his arms hanging by his sides. He took a few steps around the room to get the stiffness out of his legs and came to sit down in the chair that Virginie indicated to him.

There was, indeed, a bit of everything; rural landscapes, fore-shortened views of the roofs of Paris, quite a number of bunches of flowers and a few portraits.

'Are they your children?' Max asked.

'That's Paulo, a year ago. He's grown a lot since then. That's Garance. It's more recent. And there, they're sleeping.'

The two children's faces side by side in the middle of the piece of paper, almost touching, leaning slightly towards each other as if drawn by a magnetic force. In her efforts to depict the round-ness of their cheeks, Virginie had given them wrinkles. Max thought of a large painting of Christ that he had seen in a museum or a church, he couldn't really remember where now. Telma had stopped, transfixed, before the Virgin and Child of some Italian painter – they were in Florence, it was their first trip after their retirement. With her hand in front of her mouth, as if to avoid soiling the sacred work with her profane breath, she had whispered: 'It's magnificent!'

Max, who believed for his part that once you had seen one Virgin and Child you had seen them all, couldn't understand why his wife remained fascinated by this flat image imbued with a sadness that owed more to languor than real grief.

The child was hideous with a pouting mouth and glassy eyes, with the flaccid skin of an old man and a forehead more wrinkled than a piece of parchment. 'The Virgin and Child,' Telma said again, 'magnificent!' What on earth is there in that to titillate her? Max wondered. He knew that some Jews would have preferred to have been born Catholic, and not just for the practical reasons one might think (no pogrom, no camps, ham at every meal), but because, in some ways, they found it more refined, less garish; and the very sound of the word 'Catholic' had resonance to it like a peal of bells, a little waltz, a ditty. 'Jewish' was despatched, an onomatopoeia for flight, a sort of desperate 'Off we go.'

Telma nevertheless liked the idea of the chosen people, which she tended to think of more as a privileged club than a confession. If there had been a religion that embraced both a single god and a single follower, she would have signed herself up to it straight away. It, therefore, wasn't a mystic trance that glued her to the icon. What she liked was the wrinkled little child, old before his time, like herself. What she liked was the marvellous juxtaposition of virginity and maternity, every woman's dream, intact and productive, not submitting to any kind of invasion while still affording the luxury of escape. Good riddance, no man in the house. Like Virginie, a virgin for all infinity, Virginie.

'Virginie,' Max proclaimed solemnly.

She looked up at him and smiled, proud of her work, proud of her children.

'It's magnificent,' said Max, tapping the portraits of Paulo and Garance. 'You're a true artist.'

'Thank you, Mr Opass. I'm really touched that you should say that, you know. Especially because it's not easy getting into this line of work. I asked in the café over the road where they some-times have exhibitions whether they wouldn't take a few of my paintings and, obviously, the answer was no. Because, as far as they're concerned, I'm Mrs Lazieu, who goes and has her little cup of coffee in the mornings. They couldn't imagine that I might have something to say, a soul. People are full of prejudices, you know. The greatest artists and poets sometimes had the most stupid little jobs at the same time.'

'Quite so, Virginie, you're absolutely right.'

Max would have liked to believe what he was saying. Who was he to judge the quality of these paintings? The children looked like old people and for some that was the stamp of genius. The trees looked like trees and the green of the grass was a good likeness. Most of the bouquets of flowers wouldn't have looked out of place on a box of chocolates. As for Virginie, she obviously had a soul and plenty to say. And yet. And yet he didn't believe in them.

There was Telma again, knocking on the window of the crypt. Would Virginie be able to see her? Would she manage to portray her glow, her permanent air of defiance? Max saw her again and again, standing on a hillside, a minute perpendicular figure, a sturdy little rod. The wind rising up from the valley flattened the front panel of her long skirt against her tummy. The children were rolled up into balls at her feet, tumbling in the tender grass. Dora Steiner was walking along below her, on her husband's arm. They were surveying their property, the gardens of the presbytery that they had bought for a song by selling shirts designed by their seamstress. Slowly, Telma lifted her right arm, her eyes fixed on the line of the horizon, and put her lock of hair back in place. There was a sadness about her – this unsung designer standing steadfast in the middle of a field – that could only be exaggerated by the dazzling summer light. When the sun is overhead it beats down on the forehead, tortures the nape of the neck. Telma, a tiny vertical form, refused to languish in the heat, persisted through the immensity of the day. The needle of a pair of compasses was planted in her belly, leaving the free arm of the instrument to sweep tirelessly round the earth. Max sees all of this but doesn't know how to put it into words. He would like to explain to Virginie that this uprightness, Telma's revolt, is perfectly contained in each feature of her face, that all her life she was the point on which light converged and from which energy diverged.

'Do you see, in this photo,' he said, leaning towards her with a slide in his hand, 'the way she held her chin? Slightly raised?'

Virginie took the picture and held it up to the window.

'There?'

'No, no, come on!' cried Max. 'That one's Lisette.'

'Lisette?'

'Lisette, her friend. Anyway, it doesn't matter. I'm talking about Telma, here!'

He wanted to point out his wife's face with his finger but the white plastic frame was so small; you would have needed a pinhead to draw the outline of the people in the picture.

'So your wife is the woman next to the other one?'

'What do you mean next to? I'm telling you this is her, here, right in the middle. The one in the brown coat.'

'Ah, yes. Okay, the brown coat, yes. You can't see her hair very well.'

'Here,' said Max, taking another slide. 'On this one you can't see anything but hair. Curly, very dark. Obviously it turned white later. She always refused to dye it, you know.'

'So am I to do her with brown hair?' Virginie asked.

Max couldn't make up his mind. The five photographs that he had chosen came from different eras. They covered some forty years. He would have liked a synthesis. He thought the portrait could accomplish this miracle: to give Telma her integrity, to define what it was about her face that abolished time.

'Now you're asking.'

'You don't know what colour you want her hair?'

'I haven't thought about it. You're a practical person. You've plenty of common sense, that's very good, congratulations, but . . .'

'What if I put a hat on her!' cried Virginie, leaping up from her chair.

She was suddenly full of energy. The unthinkable had finally happened. She ended up a few crossroads back on her trajectory and she would have cheerfully chucked all the philosophers out of the window if she could have been sure that the cruel geography of fate didn't adhere to implacable laws as she had always imagined.

'A hat? why not a crown of flowers, while you're at it? No, I've explained, I want something very simple, no frills, just the face in a little gilt frame.'

'You haven't explained anything to me, Mr Opass,' said Virginie. 'I've been talking nonstop.'

'Well, there we are, I've said it now. You'll just have to give her a scarf.'

'A scarf on her head.'

'A headscarf. Don't you ever wear a headscarf?'

Virginie did a rather bewildered pout.

'Give me a scarf, a square of silk, anything that can be knotted. I'll show you.'

Virginie got to her feet, obediently, somewhat terrorised by the old man and the unexpected way in which he raised his voice and got carried away on subjects that couldn't matter less, details.

'It's not going to be easy,' she called from the wardrobe.

Why, wondered Max, didn't women wear scarves any more? What did they put on their heads when it was cold, when they went to funerals? A bonnet, a wide-brimmed hat? Some women wore baseball caps with rigid, crescent-shaped peaks. It wasn't very becoming. You couldn't see their eyes. Luckily, most of them didn't wear anything over their dishevelled hair. Bareheaded, they advanced like solitary scouts or in little battalions, with hard eyes and firm mouths, warrior-like and insolent, in Telma's image. In their day, Telma had seemed strange. Lisette was normal: gentle, friendly, welcoming, all sweetness and smiles. Like day and night, the sweet serving girl and the Amazon queen. What did they have in common? Old hypocrite, as if you didn't know.

'I warned you, these are all I've got,' said Virginie with a little piece of material in each hand.

Max frowned.

'This is the cat's bandanna,' she said, handing him a red and white handkerchief.

'The cat's bandanna? Your cat wears a scarf? But you don't?'

Virginie smiled and tried to knot the square of cotton over her head.

'No, stop,' said Max, 'you look like a pirate. Let me do it.'

He took the bandanna from her, folded it carefully in four and assessed the other piece of fabric. It was made of finely woven wool in greeny grey with little red dots here and there, it was slightly crumpled but supple and soft to the touch.

'This is the real McCoy,' said Max, as a connoisseur. 'Lelièvre made this sort of thing in the sixties. We made a very pretty little outfit in this stuff; a short jacket, three-quarter sleeves, knee-length skirt, ultra-classic, lined in silk throughout. We stopped after a month because of its cost price. Where did you get it?'

'It's Garance's noo-noo.'

'I beg your pardon?'

'It's my daughter's little cloth, she sleeps with it. She rolls it into a ball and sucks her thumb at the same time. I actually gave her a quilted nylon nightcap, it was softer. I don't know where she unearthed this thing. It's woollen, it's scratchy. I told her that it wasn't meant for children, but she's very stubborn.'

'Your daughter has good taste. There's nothing better than wool and loathing . . .' Max put his hand over his mouth and shook his head. 'I'm sorry, I meant woollen clothing.'

'Some mornings when she wakes up her cheek is all red,' Virginie said thoughtfully.

'And don't you ever wake up with one cheek all red?'

Virginie flushed scarlet, smiled and leant her head towards Max so that he could put the scarf over her head. He expertly folded the offcut along the diagonal and put it onto the young woman's clear forehead; she closed her eyes. Holding the fabric in place with his thumbs, he brought it down over her temples and her cheeks. Then he crossed the two ends over to hold her chin tightly like a pair of hands, and ran them round her neck to knot them at the back.

'Go and have a look at yourself in the mirror.'

Too impatient to see the result to go as far as the mirror above the fireplace, Virginie opened the window and pushed the pane against the wall to contemplate her reflection. She was delighted by the transformation, and her face lit up. The muted colours blended together in the blank square of glass, becoming ghostlike and indistinct. Standing behind her to admire the result, Max was overcome by an interminable shudder.

'Telma, what are you doing here? If you're coming back from the dead, are you doing it to make me happy or to make me miserable? What are you trying to say to me? Are you asking me to leave you in peace? Do you want me to carry on? Do you think this portrait should be done?'

Virginie nodded – yes, she could see what he meant, something simple, just the face in a gilt frame.

'It's fine,' she announced, 'I think I understand.'

She turned back to Max and found that the old man had his head in his hands and was looking horror-struck.

'Are you feeling all right?' she asked, guiding him to the nearest chair.

Max was incapable of answering, frozen by the hallucination.

'Here, have a little rest,' said Virginie, settling him on the sofa.

Max sank into the only-too-familiar give of the cushions. It was going to be a good hour before he would find the strength to extricate himself from them.

Frédéric and Marion

27th May 1994

My darling,

Some news from your old father Max.

You can't imagine how happy I was to get your long letter. I reread it several times. You go into so much detail. Every time that you tell me about something, it's as if I were there. By the way, when it comes to stir-fried noodles, I hope you don't mind if I say I don't need an explanation, I've already had them. Anyway, here I am criticising you when you know very well that I think the world of you and all of yours. Yes, even Yao. You see, I can read your thoughts. I know that it's very hard for mothers to understand their sons, especially when they grow up to become men. You remember him as a baby, as a little boy who cried if he couldn't see you when he came out of school, you remember when he couldn't even get himself dressed. So it's hardly surprising that this business with the vinyl trousers has got you in a state, but it's not worth it, I promise you. When we were working in the clothing industry if we'd had vinyl, I can assure you that we wouldn't have gone to all the trouble of working with leather.

Have faith in your old Max, Yao is a good boy who's just looking for ways to annoy you. It's normal, sons just do look for ways to annoy their parents. With girls it's different. We never had any problems with you. Always first in school. No point in setting any limits on you. You set them for yourself. On the other hand, your brother was another kettle of fish. Rebellion, the whole shebang, when he brought his group of pan pipers to the workshop, enough said; it's all in the past. Or maybe it's genetic, because it's different in other families.

Spare a thought for Nanou, Lisette's daughter, what a disaster! She was such a sweet little girl with ribbons in her hair, she looked like an angel. We've good reason to worry about our children. I shouldn't tell you this, you've already got enough to worry about with Mariko who's got her eye on the Nobel Prize. She's just a child still. I saw a programme the other day about the way Japanese students are overworked; it made me shudder. What is it that we're all looking for at the end of the day? Sometimes it strikes me that we should just stay at home, nice and quiet, in the warmth when it's cold outside, and only go out when it's warm, take the air and come straight back in. Life is so full of dangers. It's probably because I'm old. Tell me if you think I'm losing my marbles; you know that I can't stand senility.

I'm putting up a fight. You couldn't say that I've let myself go. I'm doing a lot of walking at the moment. Two or three hours a day. At my own pace. The weather's glorious here. Sun every day. I know the city like the back of my hand, the alleyways, the bridges, the little roads. I make out little tourist itineraries for myself. In the afternoon I go to the club, but not every day. Routines aren't good for the old.

Mme Brodsky invited me round for tea. Have I mentioned Mme Brodsky to you? I didn't accept. She's very lonely, I think, but charming. A cultivated woman, a musician perhaps. The problem is that it's such a henhouse there, they coo – or rather cluck – over every piece of gossip and tittle-tattle, and I have no desire to be the source of the gossip. I shouldn't mention this to you. But you're a big girl. You won't go dreaming up things that haven't happened. You know your father. Anyway, I've decided to give myself some time. I do a lot of thinking. Before, I used to get angry about something and then it would all be over. Crumbs swept under the carpet. Now I'm having a spring clean. I walk for hours and I think. I wouldn't be able to say what it is that I think about, and, anyway, it's a secret. We thrive on such small pleasures.

Actually, I haven't told you the best of it. Do you remember that I took out a life insurance policy? I sent you the papers so that you could tell me what you thought about it. I don't think you had time to. I'd made up my mind, anyway. What's the point of having money in the bank? I hardly spend anything. So, I made some investments. It was about a year and a half ago. With a rate of 6.5% I said to myself: 'Now's the time to invest, old man!' I had an appointment with a young girl; she was a bit boss-eyed but very kind. In just five minutes, it was all over, I was ruined, if you see what I mean. I put the whole lot aside. The funny thing is that now, just like that, there are little things that I want, nothing extravagant but, well, there's no need to live like a hermit. I've decided to terminate the contract. Except that it doesn't happen just like that, given that we're halfway through the year. They know all about taking the money, but when it comes to giving it back, there's no one there to help you! It's out of the question, they said, the money can't be touched.

I didn't let that put me off. I wrote them a little letter making out that one of my kidneys had had it. I was going to need an operation, I said, but a friend of mine who's a doctor had said that even if the operation is successful I wouldn't have more than eight months to live, or a year at best. I had, so to speak, refused the operation to save them the expense of the hospital stay; I told them that I had decided to end my days peacefully at home. Consequently *(this is how I concluded my letter) I was asking them to terminate my contract and give me back my money which would also save them the funeral expenses. As if by chance, a week later, I got my nest egg back.*

I'm managing fine, as you can see. If you speak to your brother on the telephone, give him all my news. I haven't yet answered his letter. It's odd, I always know what to write to you, but with him, not a squeak, I don't even know where to begin. Maybe fathers are just looking for ways to annoy their sons, too. No, I'm joking. I'm enclosing a decorative post card that I found on a stall along the banks of the Seine. 'Japanese cherry trees'; it reminded me of you. Are there any in the streets of Tokyo? I'll have to come and see you one day. Twenty hours in a plane is a long time, but it goes more quickly with a good book. I count it out again and again, it's exactly a quarter of a century since you left, my little poppet. Every year I said, 'We'll go next year.' Like with Jerusalem.

Your mother won't have seen your house before she died. I wonder whether it's really a good idea for me to make this journey, after all. Without her, there doesn't seem much point. And you wouldn't know what to do with me. I'd be under your feet the whole time. I don't like ending on a sad note. I'd love to tell you a good joke that I heard on the radio yesterday. But jokes are for telling; they lose all their edge when they're committed to paper. Pretend you've heard it, and look after yourself.

Hello to everyone
Big hugs from Daddy.

Max felt a tightening round his heart. It was a particularly unpleasant feeling and one that was far too familiar. He slowed down, took a deep breath, stopped, leant against the guard-rail of the bridge and watched the water flowing for a few moments. A new pain. The other times it had been like an electric shock, a long icy knifing, appallingly sharp. More like a heaviness than a pain, he said to himself as he set off again. 'With a heavy heart,' went the song. That was exactly it; one of those net bags that had been filled too full, weighing down on the handles, threatening to break and spill its contents all over the pavement. He shouldn't have posted that one either. What was Nadya going to think with his stories about Mme Brodsky?

No, that wasn't it, the handles were still tugging at him. Why did he have to go and talk about Nanou? He couldn't think about anything else at the moment. And now I've got a tummyache. No stomach problems for eighty years and now, on a lovely sunny afternoon having had soup and a slice of smoked turkey for lunch, it gets him. Cramps, nausea. He had to sit down. He would have to get to the end of the footbridge, cross the road and park himself in the first bar he came across. His eyesight was blurring, he found it difficult to walk straight.

He could see Lisette at her daughter's funeral. Poor Nanou. At the time people didn't say overdose, they said 'just like that'. She'd died just like that. Lisette was worse than dead herself. Such a kind, cheerful woman, how was it possible? He crossed the road. A car tooted at him as he struggled to get onto the pavement.

'It's green, Grandpa!' the driver shouted through his open window.

Green yourself, thought Max. But he didn't have the strength to reply. He walked round the Institut de France and set off down the rue de Seine. He walked past the galleries and the

boutiques that sold nothing that you would want to buy. Even
though the sun was still high in the sky, he felt as if night were
falling. A grey haze was rising up from the street and the
pavement.

When he had left home an hour earlier to post his letter, he
had been delighted by the inconsequential scurrying of the little
clouds; a fragrant breeze made him screw up his eyelids slightly.
Galvanised by the Parisian spring, he had got onto the number
27 without thinking. It was his bus, the one that passed just thirty
metres from his house and took him all over the place: to the
bridge club, to the Samaritaine shopping complex, to Saint-Lazare
station. It had a nice route: the Jardin de Luxembourg, along the
Seine, the Louvre, Opéra; a busy line. All of the passengers existed
in discreet and friendly complicity, conscious that they were chic
people, travelling on the best bus in the capital.

He had alighted at the Pont-Neuf. He would cross on foot,
look at the Seine to the left and the right, cast an eye over the
Place Dauphine and have a little sigh. (It was a habit that he had
adopted with Telma, turning his head briefly to the Place Dauphine and sighing. It meant: 'It's so pretty here. We'd so love to
live here! And apparently Yves Montand and Simone Signoret
live here.') He might even get as far as the big department stores
– there was always something you needed to buy if you really
thought about it.

On the second part of the bridge, he had seen a young woman
asleep on one of the round benches that adorn the little recesses
in the stone. Her hair was dirty and it clung to her head, her
eyelids were red, she had a black eye across to her right temple,
her lips were grey and chapped, and her body was covered in
disparate articles of clothing which bore the marks of various
falls, blows and meals. Max had stopped. She wasn't as much as
thirty years old. Someone is thinking about her right now, he

told himself for reassurance, a mother, a father, a sister. Someone is worried about her and will come and help her. He had watched her for a moment, powerless and sad. That was where it had started; a fist had tightened in the middle of his tummy. He had carried on on his way. The buildings of the Samaritaine rose up in front of him. Max couldn't go there now, he was thinking of the misery, of all the sadness in this vast world for which there was no remedy at all. He had walked along the quays and turned left along the passerelle des Arts, as if to erase the painful memory of his walk along the Pont Neuf.

Backtracking does not always bring as much consolation as you might hope. At the first street corner he turned right into the rue des Beaux-Arts. Such a pretty little girl, he said to himself again, and her mother was so kind, so full of joy, completely the opposite of Telma. A soft, gentle body with arms that were too short as if to pull her lover to her all the more quickly. Lisette's pretty, square face cut in two by her wide smile and full lips. The second time that he had met Telma, in a café on the Grands Boulevards where she had suggested they meet, he had caught sight of the two women, sitting at the back of the room, huddled together. They were not talking. They were looking over towards the entrance, on the watch.

'Max, can I introduce Lisette.'

He had shaken their hands and had sat down opposite them. Telma didn't say anything. She was staring at him, a smile playing on her lips. Lisette didn't stop talking, all pink under her red hair, laughing all the time and rolling her r's, as she rolled her eyes and rolled the whole of her lovely plump body. Telma knew what she was doing, she was sending her twittering friend as an advance party, an intrepid, plucky pioneer. Dressed in black, slimmer, slightly taller and infinitely more distinguished – like a girl watching her younger sister playing with her dolls with a mixture of indulgence and amused disdain – she surveyed the scene. It was she who had paid for the drinks and who had stood up to leave first.

'There's something I need to go and buy,' she had said. 'No, don't get up. Stay here in the warm. I'll come back in an hour and if you've gone, well never mind.'

An hour later they were in Lisette's room, and she was undressing, talking all the while, telling Max a thousand and one little anecdotes, while he was wondering just how to stop himself jumping on her there and then, so that she wouldn't know that he hadn't had a woman for three years, and that he had never seen one completely naked. But even naked, Lisette was exactly the same: sitting cross-legged on the bed, she prattled away gaily, accompanying her words with great arm movements that made her breasts bounce up and down.

'I'm not shy about my body. I never have been. I was posing for painters when I was fourteen. We are as we are, aren't we? God didn't invent clothes.'

She started to laugh.

Max moved towards her, and it was she who kissed him, raising herself up on her short legs. He squeezed her in his arms, gratefully.

'You're so strong!'

Making love with her was like a children's game. She laughed, chattered endlessly, made jokes, whimpered a bit, enjoyed herself so much that you could forget the consequences.

Max had married Telma a month later. Lisette was a witness. When the time came to sign the register, she gave a little wink to her lover of one day. I had to choose one of them, he thought, vaguely remembering a fable in which two young girls fought over a bear's heart. In fact, he hadn't chosen anything at all; Telma had simply been more determined, and sadder, too. And how could you resist any woman's sadness, when you can't help yourself wanting to save her from it?

A few years later, when they had gone off to the woods for a picnic – him, Telma and their children, Lisette, Paul (her husband) and the adorable Nanou – Lisette had suggested he went for a walk along the river bank with her.

'Those two oldies are watching the children,' she had said, taking Max's hand, 'we can go for a walk.'

Telma and Paul – she immersed in an exciting book, and he lost in a bottomless reverie – hadn't turned a hair. As for the children, they were digging holes in the ground, trying to find the biggest earthworm in the world.

When they came to the water's edge, Lisette had lain down in the tall grass.

'Make love to me, Max.'

'You're married, Lisette.'

'So are you, my darling.'

'Well, no then.'

'But why not?'

'You know very well. Because we're married, it's just not done.'

'That's not a reason, Max,' Lisette had said sulkily. 'We were married to each other before we got married to the two others.'

'We slept together, it's not quite the same.'

'For me, you were the first, that's more important than any marriage.'

'The first?' said Max.

'Nearly,' Lisette murmured.

Her eyes were full of tears. With her head among the bulrushes, she bit her fists.

'Paul isn't much fun,' she said, crying.

'Neither is Telma, you know.'

'Is that true?'

'What do you think?'

Lisette had got to her feet, she had held Max in her arms and whispered in his ear:

'With us, we're married for ever, not even death can come between us.'

He had patted her shoulder kindly and led her back.

When they arrived within sight of the group, Nanou was sitting astride her father's chest and was teasing him, touching the end of his nose with a worm. Paul lay with his arms outstretched and was laughing uncontrollably.

'She only loves him,' Lisette had said, indicating her daughter.

Max lifted the collar of his coat. He was frozen. At the end of the road to the left there was a bistro. He rummaged through his pockets – what an idiot! He had forgotten his wallet. His head was spinning. Despite the dazzling mid-afternoon light, he had trouble distinguishing the ground from the buildings, the roofs from the windows, he felt as if he were walking on his hands. The sun smacked onto the white stone and left the corners and the gutters in shadow. The succession of arcades seemed like a series of dark caves. The violence of the contrast annihilated any colour; the white light was like a slap in the face, blinding; the darkness swallowed up any relief.

In front of him lay the courtyard of the Beaux-Arts Academy. He had difficulty getting across it, hoping to find a bench there, an edge in the wall or a prominent piece of stone that he could rest against. Infinitely tired, strangled by the inexplicable resurgence of long-forgotten images, he moved as if in a night-mare, seeming to take steps backwards in a peculiar perspective which illustrated a completely different life for him.

Lisette had only survived her daughter's death by a few years, each day falling further back into a childhood that she had only left inadvertently. Paul had become a little more deeply lost in his thoughts, until he finally disappeared to be reunited with his one true love, the little girl who had brought him a new treasure every day: a bottle top, a butterfly wing, a glass pebble polished by the sea. Then, a door had been closed on them once and for all. Telma had lost her little sister and he his secret love, his clowning girlfriend; he had sometimes told himself: 'When we're really old and none of this matters any more, I'll rock her in my arms and I'll tell her that she too was the first for me, nearly.'

'Are you our model?'

A boy's voice made Max jump. He had taken refuge in a dilapidated cloister peopled with marble statues with legs, arms and heads missing. He was sitting on the edge of the central fountain, staring at his open palms.

'Sorry?' he said, looking up.

A boy and a girl were standing in front of him. He was puny and blond, his brown eyes edged with long black lashes, he had a delicate childlike mouth and was dressed like a scarecrow. She was taller with a fuller figure, a colossus with sparkling blue eyes, a resplendent complexion and luxuriant black hair.

'Are you the model?' asked the girl.

'I'm so sorry,' said Max.

It was at that moment that he understood where he was. 'Beaux-Arts' was not just the name of the road, or a bus stop, it was a school of fine art and in front of him were two of the students. Max explained to them that there had been a mistake and he thanked them all the same, because he had never imagined that he could serve as a model to anyone.

'It's quite often old people, well, I mean, older people,' explained the girl.

Max looked around him at the statues in the cour du Mûrier. They represented warriors, nymphs and goddesses, young harmoniously-proportioned bodies. The women's thighs were slender, their breasts high, their bellies smooth and round; the men's muscles protruded beneath the mineral perfection of their skin. They were clearly more than a hundred years old, or antiques good and proper. Max was not very well versed in the history of art, but he was not ignorant of anatomy. There was nothing very inspiring about an old man's body with a sunken belly and in-turned hip-bones, vertebrae that stuck out and flesh that sagged. 'Times change,' he told himself. The canons of beauty could well have evolved towards some new definition without his realising it.

'And yet,' he ventured, relieved to escape from his ghosts, 'older people aren't as beautiful, though, are they?'

He made a sweeping movement with his arm, indicating the statues he had been admiring.

The students exchanged a glance.

'Beauty isn't really the problem,' said the boy.

Max looked perplexed. For him it always had been. How did you attain it, capture it, keep a hold on it? If beauty didn't count any more, what was there to replace it?

'You've lost me, young man.'

The boy shrugged his shoulders and the girl launched into a convoluted explanation. According to her, beauty was their worst enemy. To hear her getting heated on the subject, you could believe that the country was at war. Every mirror should be smashed on the spot. When he heard these words, Max couldn't help himself calling to mind the second commandment; 'Thou shalt not make any graven image . . . of any thing that is in heaven above, or in the earth beneath'. The wrath of Abraham against those who adore idols. So much violence to obtain purity.

The young girl went on to declare that we needed to free ourselves from representation. Max wondered exactly which rabbinical school she came from. It was only when she concluded with the argument that modernity was going through a period of improvisation and memory loss that he gave up on his analogy. What was it to him? What little he knew of religion was lost in the thick fog of childhood hours spent dreaming out of the window.

'You know,' said the boy, 'models aren't very well paid, and it's time-consuming. There aren't many volunteers. We make the most of what we get.'

Max felt ridiculous. To these youngsters, he was just a cheap commodity, a body that had been deserted by its vigour and couldn't even prostitute itself any longer. How would this pair go about it if he asked them to paint a portrait of Telma? They would probably start by looking for the furthest thing from them, as unmoved by her face as by a bowl of fruit standing on a cloth. A still life. He would have to explain to them that the old are as unfamiliar with death as the young, to remind them that roots are still buried in the earth, that rivers have no choice but to flow from their sources, towards their estuaries. Virginie was right: time and space. The only difference derived from the shrinking of space. Time did not exist. Max only had to close his eyes to feel the pains of his youth and the joys of his childhood.

He thought about Mr Mirallez, the gardener at the convalescent home where Telma had spent one of the last months of her life. He was a stocky man with short limbs. He had a bald head, pale drooping eyes and a very straight nose. When he smiled, his thick lips revealed two rows of perfect teeth. After a quarter of an hour of digging, he would stand up and push his closed fists into the small of his back. His kindness was legendary. You could ask anything of him: unloading shopping, accompanying those who were on their own for a walk, and even looking after children who were bored by visiting the sick.

One morning, three boys that he was looking after had had fun jumping on the branches of a thick shrub. It was a strange conifer that grew horizontally, spreading out like a peacock's tail. The children took a few steps to build up speed before jumping and then they leapt, sometimes disappearing completely in the densely covered branches. Mr Mirallez leant on his spade and watched them. From the window Max couldn't see whether he was smiling or angry. As he had taken to passing the time of day with Telma by telling her what was going on in the garden, he described the scene to her and asked what she thought of it. 'He lost his wife five years ago,' she said as if this information constituted an element of reply. 'And his son two years later. If you want my opinion, he couldn't really care less about that flattened Christmas tree of his.'

Max wasn't convinced. Without knowing what it was that made him take the story to heart, he decided to go and mention it to the relevant authorities. 'The young should learn to respect the work of the old. People shouldn't abuse the kindness of others.' He went to the reception desk to complain to the manageress on duty.

She had laughed. 'Don't worry about it. Mr Mirallez loathes that clumpy thing. He's been talking about replacing it with a hydrangea for several years.'

Max went and had a little walk round the garden. He would have liked to start up a conversation with the gardener, but what would they have talked about? You can't ask after the family of a widower who has lost his only son. So he stayed on the gravel path, his head ringing with the children's shrieks.

When he went back up to her room, he found Telma asleep with her head next to the pillow. Having settled her back on the pillow, he went back to the window and saw Mr Mirallez digging furiously. Just beyond the shrub which was reverberating with children's cries, were three large holes. The gardener was just finishing tamping down the sides of a fourth. The holes must have been a good metre long, by fifty centimetres wide. 'Why four graves?' wondered Max, 'there are only three children.' Terrified, he had closed the window again and sat down on the chair at the foot of Telma's bed, with his head in his hands.

'Aren't you on your way to a lesson?' he asked.

'Anatomy, it's compulsory in the first year,' said the girl, 'but after that . . .'

'With you, if something's not compulsory, you don't do it,' said the boy.

The girl bit her lip.

'Don't let him bully you,' said Max. 'What are your names?'

'I'm Marion and he's Frédéric.'

'Pleased to meet you,' said Max, holding out a hand that they shook shyly.

He had suddenly decided to place an order with them. There is no such thing as fate either, he decided. They will do this portrait for me. I've nothing to lose, after all. The question was knowing how to introduce the idea. He would have to be friendly, gain their confidence. The rest would come naturally.

'Who loves best can punish best,' he declared. 'Do you know that proverb? Lovers, true lovers, are always cruel.'

Frédéric and Marion started to laugh. It was a good sign.

'We're not together,' said the boy. 'We're just friends.'

'You two are friends? You can think what you like. I'm going to give you a good piece of information: a man cannot be friends with a woman. Never.'

'Well, we prove that he can,' replied Frédéric.

'Never, I tell you. It's stupid. I don't even want to talk about it,' said the old man stubbornly.

The task was proving more arduous than he had thought.

Had Lisette been his friend? She had been Telma's friend, yes. Hours spent drinking tea and discussing the recipe for choux pastry. Afternoons in the park exchanging three meaningless sentences, the same as the previous Saturday and the following Saturday. And the children? How are the children? You know it wasn't measles, after all? Really? An allergy, the doctor said. An allergy to what? We don't know that; that's the problem.

Petty little quarrels like two sparrows fighting over bread-crumbs. The women with the women and the men with the men. He would be playing chess with Paul without saying a word. He moved his pawns quickly, thinking just two moves ahead, no more. Paul had to win. But sometimes it wasn't so easy keeping the game in his adversary's favour. Not that Max was any more adept, rather because Paul, thanks to his hesitations and agonized calculations, ended up losing the thread of his strategy.

To avoid scuppering his partner, Max had gone as far as 'accidentally' knocking over the chessboard. What was he afraid of? That, by losing a game, Paul would realise everything else that he had lost? That by acknowledging Max's superiority with these little pieces of wood, he would discover that he surpassed him in love too? Nothing that precise, really. Max was only moved by a ridiculous desire for symmetry, the baseline of aesthetic aspiration, the reassuring image of the needle on a set of scales condemned eternally to pointing towards the zenith.

'And even between people of the same sex,' he said finally, 'I'm not sure there's ever real friendship.'

They arranged to meet at midday. When he had suggested ten o'clock, he had seen Frédéric and Marion's eyes growing to the size of saucers. Let's go for midday, Max had replied. He would have a snack at around ten o'clock, just to avoid being famished when he arrived. The deal was simple: Marion would take care of the portrait and, in exchange, Max agreed to let Frédéric film him on video.

'What will I have to do?'

'Nothing. Well, nothing special. You're just there, in front of the camera. You might talk, you might not say anything. We'll see. It mustn't be premeditated. That's exactly what makes it interesting, the instantaneous, but seen over a period of time. The tape moves on but you stay still.'

'I'll just have to act naturally,' Max had said, picking up on an expression he had heard on television.

'No, definitely not. I mean, not necessarily. I am stealing your image. You agree to the theft, but the infraction is still there. It's all part of it.'

Max was full of doubt. He was still quite young for his age, but from there to being a film star . . . it struck him as being a big step.

'But do you think people will like it?'

'Which people?'

'The people who watch the tape.'

'That's beside the point. No one might ever see it. Except if I include it in my final-year project. Either way, what really matters is the act itself. It's an experimental piece of work.'

Frédéric spoke to him as others might speak to children, or animals, convinced that their listener was not fully equipped to understand.

'Experimental,' Max repeated.

Then the light dawned. He gave an enigmatic little laugh. Frédéric was a hippie, like Basile. Max wouldn't have been able to put his finger on the exact basis of this brotherhood; a mixture of vagueness and technical detail, a degree of aloofness combined with tremendous vulnerability. The two boys had many common points: first and foremost the negligent way in which they dressed; they spoke a great deal about work and fairly little about themselves, valued arrogance more highly than candour, and silenced their own opinions to fall back on slogans.

'So, is that OK?' Frédéric asked.

To give her friend's request more weight, Marion had fallen to her knees in front of Max, and had joined her hands.

'It's OK,' said Max, 'I know all about hippies.'

'About what?'

'Marion, I'm relying on you,' was all the answer Max gave.

The young woman had got back to her feet and slapped her hand into the one that the old man held out to her.

'Deal.'

They had parted company as the sun began to sink. Max felt light. He thought he was managing incredibly well, and believed that things had taken a turn for the better. And he really liked this couple that wasn't a couple. The moody boy and the bombastic girl. Modern young women were fascinating. They slipped effortlessly from a slap on the back to a fluttering of eyelashes, from striding about like dock-workers to delicately putting straight the shoulder strap of a bra. They were a synthesis of everything that he had known, with something else added on top. Rancour and sadness were just baggage inherited from their mothers; their eyes were wide open, and they shone with an unprecedented strength.

The next day, he left home at ten o'clock having gulped down some instant soup, and he decided to stop by with Angus to see how the work was coming along. He wasn't in the habit of making surprise calls on people, but what could he do? He had been up since half past six in the morning. If he carried on going round in circles at home, he was in danger of having a relapse. He didn't want to telephone; there might not be anyone or, worse, there might be an answering machine. Angus might also ask him to come by later. No, he had to jump up and go without thinking about it. The journey to Butte-aux-Cailles would easily use up twenty minutes. You don't spit in the face of that sort of opportunity to kill time.

It was Diane who opened the door. She had a child at the breast and she smiled at him when he apologised for disturbing her so early.

'Angus isn't here,' she said, 'but come in, please.'

She sat down on the floor, with her back against the wall, and carried on nursing the baby. The breast which emerged from her white blouse was perfectly smooth and round. The walls of the studio were bare. In places the pieces of black tape remained, indicating the departure of the sketches they had held. Max settled himself in the armchair once Diane had insisted that he stayed. Through one of the fanlights that was open up near the ceiling, you could hear pigeons cooing. Max sighed, contemplating this new and very unusual Madonna.

'I didn't know you had a child,' he said.

'She's our fourth,' replied Diane. 'The others are at school. You don't mind that I'm . . .'

Max shook his head. As a child he had seen his older sisters breastfeeding, and his young aunt. As he was the youngest, he was under the women's skirts all morning. The acid smell of milk mixed with the babies' stools constituted for him the only perfume of true happiness. With Telma it had been different. After Nadya was born she had been exhausted. With her hand in the small of her back one minute and wiping her forehead the next, she had wandered around their little apartment, complicating her life with pointless tasks. He remembered one stifling August morning when Telma had been lying prostrate on the sofa, her red eyes underlined by dark rings. Nadya was yelling in her cradle. Max was about to get up to get the baby, when he noticed two dark circles on his wife's blouse. 'Look,' he said, 'Nadya's screaming and it's your breasts that are crying.' Telma had looked down to her chest and had started to laugh.

'Angus has gone to Caen,' said Diane. 'He took your sketches with him. He must be afraid that I'll touch them.'

'Are you a painter too?' Max asked on the off chance.

'I'm a sculptor,' replied Diane. 'You see that behind you there. That's my work.'

Max turned his head and saw a steel girder, slightly twisted in places, standing a few metres away from him. Until then he had thought that it was a means of supporting the studio roof. He almost asked: 'What is it meant to be?' but he knew that that wasn't the right question. He was learning. Abstraction. There is more to life than representation. In order to avoid making a blunder, he threw himself in at the deep end.

'What happened to you?' he asked.

He had fallen from a small mistake into the most complete indiscretion.

Diane smiled.

'The only person who has ever asked me that question – apart from you, I mean – is Angus. I married him within a week.'

'Watch out,' said Max, relieved, 'my heart is there for the taking.'

'I don't mind telling my story, but people are embarrassed, they don't like to ask. They're obsessed by it, I can see it in their eyes. They just don't have the courage. I've always been like this. Well, let's say it happened very early on. It's my own fault, I can't blame anyone. I wanted to see what was in a saucepan.'

She stopped talking for a moment, rested the baby against her shoulder and tapped her back. Her naked breast looked at Max, like a second face, more expressive than the first, its youth unaltered. The old man couldn't help himself smiling at this thought. Diane laid the baby in the crook of her elbow to offer her the other breast.

'Apart from the pain,' she carried on, 'I didn't suffer at all. It sounds odd to say it like that, but it's true. I can remember the physical pain to this day. The worst pain you could imagine. My body was floating God knows where, lagging behind me. And my face, like the head of a comet, turned red and then white, hurtling through the endless darkness around it. I kept my eyes shut for six months. When I opened them again it was evening. No, it was daytime, but my father had closed the curtains. I saw two shapes bending over me. My parents, like two suns that I couldn't make out. They said my name, several times, so gently, so softly, and I knew that I was saved. They were wonderful. I lived a very protected life, like a sort of Burmese princess, sheltered from other people's stares, in a white room, with lace-edged sheets, lead crystal chandeliers and pictures on the walls. I never went to school. My mother taught me everything. We wrote together, did sums together and we sewed too. We would sit down before a great mountain of multicoloured moiré ribbons with iridescent borders, remnants of velvet, feathers and rolls of crisp organdie, and we would set to work. She made theatre costumes.'

The baby gave a little cough and seemed to choke. Max, terrified, wanted to get up; but Diane lifted her up calmly, stroked her back and her head, and, having closed her blouse, laid the baby along her thighs facing her.

'Miss Molly is too greedy,' she said, passing her index fingers through her daughter's closed fists.

While she carried on talking she started to rock her legs gently and regularly. After two silent solemn yawns, the child fell into a deep sleep.

'For a long time, the only people I met were doctors. All terribly kind. I was their little darling, their beloved little guinea pig. They did an enormous amount of work on my face. I realise,' she said, laughing, 'that it doesn't really show. But I've come a very long way and then, when I was ten, I asked them to stop. I'd had enough of being put to sleep for nothing. My parents didn't insist. They told me that if they loved me as I was, there would surely be other people who were susceptible to my charms. That's their kind of humour. They're very amusing. When I was seventeen, I enrolled in a sculpture class. Angus was standing there with a paint brush in his mouth, a cigarette behind his ear and an axe in his hand. I was walking along the street and I stopped to look at a poster in the window. The studio was on the street. I saw this man in a white room, he looked disorientated. I was curious. I went in and said: "I'd like to enrol for the sculpture class." He looked at me and said: "You've got a pretty funny face, haven't you!" and I told him that a man who had a paint brush in his mouth, a cigarette behind his ear and an axe in his hand wasn't really in a position to comment. He laughed. Angus laughs a lot. It's a blessing.'

'What a beautiful story!' said Max.

'Better than a top model. That's what I tell my children to comfort them. As they get older they start to suffer on my behalf. But you didn't come to hear this.'

Perhaps I did, Max thought to himself. Perhaps I came to look truth in the face, whatever it looked like.

'Oh, you know, at my age, you've got time to spare.'

He backtracked immediately, embarrassed.

'I'm sorry. I don't mean I've wasted my time listening to you.

Quite the opposite. What I meant was when you get old you set yourself goals willy-nilly, just to give yourself something to do. You're at the end of the reel. The thread doesn't unwind as easily as it used to. You have to give it a bit of help. I worked in the rag trade for more than thirty years, and I now realise that it's like a metaphor for life. God, I'm pompous, it's terrible!'

'No, go on, carry on, I love anything to do with fabric,' said Diane.

'Well, clothes are like life. It takes a long time, and a lot of patience and detail to make them. If you botch it at the tacking stage, you can be sure it'll pinch on the seams. If you save on thread putting the buttons on, they'll fall off when it's worn for the first time. You take trouble, you follow the pattern, you take care over the lining and then one day, the garment is finished. Then it gets worn, and that's it.'

Max felt a wave of sadness surging back over him.

'Except that no one's ever seen a suit get a dress pregnant,' said Diane.

'You're sharper than I am. I put together these great sentences but I always end up tripping myself up.'

'It's the albatross complex,' she said.

'The whaty what?'

'Don't you know "The Albatross"? His giant wings are so cumbersome he cannot walk. It's a Baudelaire poem about someone like you, someone who trips himself up as you call it.'

'Ah yes, Baudelaire, a classic,' said Max.

He felt ridiculous. A classic, that didn't mean anything.

'Yes, it is,' said Diane. 'That's exactly it. A classic, that's someone who manages to pin an expression on something that has existed for thousands of years. A classic is the one who puts the full stop at the end of it. That's probably why my husband loves and loathes the classics. He loves them because they're reassuring.

He loathes them because he's too flexible himself to succumb to that sort of authority. It's maddening.'

Diane smiled at Max. Now that he had become accustomed to her face, he knew how to interpret her grimaces. Her smooth youthful voice was reassuring. As she spoke her hands danced in front of her chest. Her eyes, which had remained intact, allowed glimpses of her archaic beauty, a life that had been buried, a minute Pompeii. Perhaps he had spoken too soon after all. Friendship was possible between men and women. But the man had to be old and the woman burned. Yes, that was it. The exception that confirms the rule. If she were hideous to look at and he no longer had the strength, then it could happen. And how wonderful that was! An unexpected gentleness, a primitive feeling, transparent as amber, with the surprise of discovering the fossil within – how lucky! – perfectly preserved, pristine after thousands of years under flows of lava, frozen water, avalanches of sand and filthy mud. But Diane wasn't hideous, she had a funny face and magnificent breasts. But he was not without strength, his blood still burned and his heart beat faster when he saw a pretty woman. There goes my only theory, Max said to himself gaily.

'I'm going to leave you, Diane,' he said. 'I've got a little meeting.'

'A heart there for the taking, I know,' said the young woman.

Max, having gestured to her to stay sitting, blew her a kiss.

'It's for Miss Molly,' he specified before closing the door.

The young are pitiless, thought Max, as he toiled up the five floors of the dark grey building on the rue Moret. He had spent the first years of his time with Telma in a similar building. On the other side of République, in the tenth Arrondissement. The same sad, indefinable colour on the outside. The wooden front door that goes out onto the street is just a single door, the steps are uneven and some of the risers are cracked, there's a smell of cabbages, onions, chips and cooked tomatoes, with undertones of dirty socks and washing that can't ever get truly dry. The walls in the stairwell are now daubed with graffiti and pictures, some of which are obscene. As you climb higher, the light becomes stronger in the narrow spiral. From the fourth floor onwards, a huge fresco unfurls from floor to ceiling, gigantic tropical plants stretching up, shimmering in the intermittent reflections of sunlight. A tree in the courtyard, probably. A big tree as tall as the building whose leaves and branches are tossed by the whims of the wind and sketch a lacework of moving shadows.

At the time he didn't mind living in that sort of place. Telma claimed that there were rats in the stairwell, but he had never seen any. It was just after the war, you didn't ask for much, you wanted so little; you were there and that in itself was almost too much. People had lived in huts, in holes in the ground, in the woods, in cowsheds and muckheaps, they had taken food from farmyard dogs and bitten into unidentified roots that were so bitter that they made you grind your teeth; so a one-room apartment under the roofs of Paris with sunshine in the morning and running water in the courtyard was paradise.

But in the present day, in the age of automatic lifts with special compartments for coffins, it smacked of misery. He would give them a bit of money; he would force them to accept it.

'Frédéric, it's Max,' said Marion as she opened the door. 'Wait a minute, I'll get a chair down for you,' she added.

Max looked up and saw that all the furniture, the table, chairs and even the television, were hung from the ceiling on a system of pulleys. The young girl grabbed one of the red ropes which was attached to a hook on the wall, and ran it down slowly.

'The red ones are for the chairs,' she explained, 'the green

93

ones for the tables, well, I mean the table, the blue one is for the TV, and the yellow ones are for the plants.'

Max smiled admiringly.

'And the bed, what do you do for the bed?'

'It's in the next room. Fré-dé-ric,' yelled Marion, 'are you coming or what?'

'Hanging from the ceiling, too?'

'Who?'

'The bed,' said Max.

'No, no, it's on the floor. It was too complicated.'

'In my time,' said the old man, 'we had stowable beds, do you know what I mean? You lifted them up in the morning and, hey presto, they disappeared into the wall like a cupboard.'

'My great aunt had one like that,' said Marion. 'Do sit down.'

The young girl brought down two more chairs and the table.

'Would you like a cup of tea?' she asked.

'I'd love one.'

She put the water on to boil on a hotplate that was attached to the wall.

'Hello.'

Frédéric came out of the bedroom, his hair tousled and his eyes half closed.

'Did I wake you up?' the old man asked.

'No, no, I was in the photo lab.'

Max wondered how many rooms this minute apartment boasted.

The session went on for more than an hour. Frédéric started by setting up the video camera while Max drank his tea from a chipped bowl.

'Are these the only photos you've got?' asked Marion, who had installed herself at the table to scrutinize the laser enlargements that Max had taken the precaution of having made right at the beginning of this undertaking, on the advice of Mr Jacques, his bookseller.

Mr Jacques had explained to him that colour photocopies were an excellent option, they were quick, clean and modern. He had just invested in a machine that took up half his shop.

'I've got rid of the books,' Mr Jacques had said. 'I only kept the dictionaries. Anyway, it's only the kids from school who come and buy the books on their curriculum. There was no point in cluttering the place up with them. Two or three new publications to put in the window, the prize-winners when the literary prizes are announced, cookery books for Christmas and there you have it. You know the bakery next door is going to sell? I've submitted my file to the bank. If I manage to get the funds together, I'm going to open a multimedia complex,' Mr Jacques had announced proudly. 'You have to move with the times.'

'I'm sure you do,' Max had replied, handing him the five dog-eared snaps some of which had gone slightly green.

'Are you going to make a montage?'

'No, they're for my personal use,' Max had answered evasively.

The bookseller had not pursued the question, delighted as he was to be inaugurating his new toy.

'Come and have a look, Fred,' said Marion.

'Hang on, I can't get this stand to open.'

'Oh, come on. Leave the stupid stand.'

Max sat motionless in his chair, wondering what was so exciting.

'Look there, you see how her face is hazy? The picture's actually focused on the camel's eye.'

Frédéric leant over the table and smiled.

'And this one, completely overexposed.'

'Did you take them?' the boy asked.

'Yes,' said Max, torn between modesty and shame.

'They're not bad,' said Frédéric admiringly. 'They're raw.'

He settled himself back behind the camera and didn't say another word.

Max, paralysed, wondered whether the filming had started. He hardly dared breathe. His eyes wandered all over the room only to end up inevitably in the bottomless chasm of the lens. After a few minutes he allowed himself a question.

'What would you like me to do?'

Frédéric didn't reply. With his eye clamped to the other end of the contraption he made an energetic swirling movement with his left hand which could have meant 'turn yourself round,' 'carry on speaking' or 'move back'. Not knowing what to do, Max looked at Marion who had secured a rope across the room and was hanging up the five reproductions with clothes pegs. He admired the delicate way in which the young girl took her perfectly sharpened pencils from her pencil case. She spread several thick sheets of paper in front of her, and they rustled softly as they slid over the table.

'First of all, I'm going to do a few sketches,' she explained to the old man. 'I don't want too hard an outline.'

'That's just what I thought you'd do,' said Frédéric, 'a good, careful piece of work.'

Max wondered what the boy had against good, careful work. The note of irony had not escaped him.

When Dastier had turned up one morning at the clothing workshop, he'd taken pleasure in unthreading needles, and pulling the tacked garments apart. Victor Steiner was dead and it was his cousin by marriage who was taking over the business. 'A modern man,' as he liked to describe himself. With him, there was no question of playing the little Jewish tailor: 'I'm not racist,' he was at pains to add, 'but the old man's ways have had their time, nowadays you machine stitch straight away.' The staff, from

the designers to the finishers, had stared at him round-eyed.
What did this boy know about machine stitching? And what did
he mean by 'Jewish tailor'? Marie-Jo, Fernande, Albert and Liouba
had all been christened in church. 'With me, you're going to go
into mass-production. My rate is twenty items a day, with
machined hems, a couple of stitches at the shoulder for the lining
and bang! bang! bang! put it to bed. I sell, they buy, they chuck
away, I sell again. Clever, isn't it?' The new boss accompanied
his speech with long conspiratorial looks at the youngest of the
employees. 'No more overtime!' he shouted, 'we're in the Twentieth Century, for goodness' sake.' This had left Max in pensive
mood. The Twentieth Century meant running up flimsy things
that could be thrown away as soon as possible so that you could
go and buy more. Dastier called this a new philosophy of life.
Why not? This was a world whose laws were infinitely more
simple than in the one he had just buried. The goal was clear
and simple, it was a question of gain; not of accumulation. It
was healthy, like a giant body that filled itself and voided itself
several times a day. They'd just have to make bigger dustbins.
There was no point in having a revolution over such a small
point.

'Do you live together?' Max asked suddenly.

'Yes,' Frédéric and Marion replied in unison.

'And do you ... how shall I put this? I'm sorry to be so
indiscreet. You don't have to answer, but ... you sleep together?'

'Exactly,' said the boy.

Max wondered what sort of corrupt hormones coursed in their
veins.

'And if, and I mean if,' he continued maliciously, 'one of you
has an affair.'

'An affair?' Frédéric repeated as if it were the funniest thing
he had ever heard.

'We come to an arrangement,' said Marion. 'We do it in shifts.'

Shifts, thought Max. He wasn't sure he wanted to know any more about this sort of behaviour.

'Could you read this?' Frédéric asked, handing a piece of paper to the old man without taking his eye from the viewfinder. 'It's a list of words. You won't have any rehearsal. You'll just discover them as you read through it. Out loud. As quickly as you like . . . No, not like that. Hold the paper normally. There's no point in hiding yourself. No one's pretending you know the list by heart; what I'm filming is you reading a list.'

Max obediently started to read, taking care to pronounce each word clearly.

'Slate, conqueror, toy, doorway, jacket . . .'

He stopped.

'What's going on now?' asked Frédéric, rather irritated. 'Don't tell me it's illegible. Go on, Max. We'll never get this done if you don't put a bit of effort into it.'

'I'm quite happy to put some effort into it,' said Max, 'but I can't pronounce this word.'

'Which word?'

'The one after "jacket".'

'Marion, what comes after "jacket"? Can you have a look please?'

The young girl got up with a sigh and read the word that the old man pointed out to her with his finger.

'Pupil,' she announced.

'You can't read "pupil"? You've got to be joking?' said Frédéric, laughing.

'No, sir. I can't.'

'It's not even a swear word.'

'I'm not afraid of swear words,' Max replied with an air of pride. 'But I don't say that word.'

98

'Why?'

'Because of my accent.'

Marion, who had gone back to her work, stopped what she was doing and turned towards the old man.

'It's true, you've got an accent. It's a very nice one, actually. You shouldn't be ashamed of an accent. It's your culture. We all have accents. To someone from Marseilles, I have a Parisian accent.'

'I'm not ashamed. It's just that with my accent this word doesn't sound like anything.'

Frédéric wasn't saying anything. He zoomed in on the old man's face.

'Where's your accent from?' Marion asked.

'Oh, it's complicated,' said Max.

'Go on, be nice. If you tell us where your accent is from we'll take "pupil" off the list.'

Max smiled. He rather liked Marion. He might as well be honest, he had always preferred women.

'It's a Russian accent,' he said. 'Well, Yiddish really. Russian Jewish.'

'Are you Jewish?' the young girl exclaimed.

'Why not?' said the old man, folding the list in four.

'So you did the . . . the Holocaust?' she asked with a look of amazement.

Max burst out laughing.

'No, it wasn't me, it was them.'

Marion watched him slapping his thighs as he dissolved laughing. She threw Frédéric an inquisitive look, but he was completely absorbed in his work.

'It must have been horrible,' she said, her arms hanging useless by her sides, feeling sorry that she didn't want to laugh about it and mortified that she didn't want to cry about it either.

'Yes, it certainly was,' replied Max once he had calmed down. 'Really, completely, utterly horrible.'

'Do you think about it all the time?'

'In fact, no,' Max replied after a while. His face darkened. 'I wasn't there myself.'

Marion was staring at him, confused.

'At the beginning of the war, I enlisted in the French Army and I was taken prisoner. My wife's first husband died over there. In the camps,' he added. 'Auschwitz-Birkenau, have you heard of it?'

He remained thoughtful for a while. There was not a sound in the room. Marion was watching him, her mouth half open, blinking continuously. She had that look in her eye that he knew well, the one Nadya had as a child when he told her the story of Little Red Riding Hood. 'The pretty little girl was walking through the woods, picking flowers and mushrooms. She was in no hurry to get to her grandmother's house. She didn't know that two big eyes were watching her from behind a tree.' At this point in the story, it worked every time, Nadya would screw herself up, bringing her knees up to her chest, lowering her head between her shoulders, and would ask: 'Whose big eyes?' Max would take a deep breath and would suddenly jump with his arms above his and shout 'The big bad WOLF!' The story he was about to tell was no children's fairy tale. The grandmother did not come back out of the animal's belly singing happily to embrace her pretty little Red Riding Hood.

'Telma, my wife, had a strange theory,' he said eventually.

What was the point in frightening this young girl. She was already so frightened; and, anyway, this wasn't something you talked about. He would get out of it with an anecdote.

'She would say: "It's like oil on water. The lighter substance rises to the surface." Her first husband was pretty heavily built, he was quite an old man with a big tummy. "Do you understand," she would ask me, "it's all a question of weight. He was old and heavy. He went straight down. Some, who were younger and lighter, managed to get out, it's like oil on water." '

'Oh shit!' shouted Frédéric. 'It's not filming any more, the tape finished at least five minutes ago.'

Nina

My dear son,

Some news from your father.

I hope you'll forgive your old father for this delay. I did get your letter and it filled me with joy. You seem to be very taken with your work. That's quite normal. Work is every man's passion. Look at me, I haven't stopped since I retired. I always find something to do and, when my imagination lets me down, life takes it upon itself to invent little problems for me. Do you know the proverb: 'The housewife didn't have enough to keep her busy so she bought herself some little piglets.' It loses a lot in translation, but you see what I mean.

Recently, I've had a new project on my mind. I want to have a portrait of your mother done. An oil painting. Something tasteful and discreet, like her. I've met a number of artists, really interesting people. At the moment I haven't had much in the way of results but I'm patient. I haven't mentioned it to your sister. You can probably guess why, I'm afraid she'll worry about it. She's very sensitive and I don't think she would really understand this whole business. She's too rational, there, that's what it is. She weighs things up for weeks before undertaking the least thing. It's quite normal, she's got a lot of responsibilities and she's very like her mother.

Level-headed Women Incorporated, that's what we've got in this family. Do you see what I mean. If I tell her that I've had meetings with painters and that I've given them a commission, she'll go crazy. 'How can you put your trust in strangers? How much did they ask you?'

I know there won't be a problem with you. You're impulsive. Is that what you call it? A true hippie. Free will and the whole shebang. Mind you, I'm the same. I remember when I decided to join the Young Communists. How old would I have been? Thirteen? Fourteen at the most. It was in '32. I went out onto the street because I'd heard some noise, and I saw some sort of demonstration march going past right in front of the house. There were red flags and closely packed rows of people forging past me. 'What on earth's this?' I asked myself. At one point, a boy left the ranks to do up his shoe lace. He knelt down for a moment and then set off at a run to join the procession again. He was the same age as me. I thought I wanted to be like him. Why do you make one decision and not another? That particular mystery's an old chestnut you can chew over for quite a while. It was different when I left the Party. But you know that story. Then I had my reasons, very good reasons even, no-one was surprised. Even so, when your mother used to knot red hankies round your neck at the beginning of each autumn to stop you getting sore throats, I used to feel a twinge of sadness. I used to watch you out of the window. You wouldn't hold anyone's hand, you always used to walk a couple of paces in front, with your nose in the air. Your sister held your mother's arm, quite the young lady already. You didn't turn to look at them. You slunk on ahead tensely like an animal. What were you dreaming of then? I stayed behind the window thinking: 'That's me, that little boy heading off to school with his red scarf.' I knew full well that you were my son, that it was now your turn to walk to school without looking back even once at your mother. A real 'tough guy'.

Nina

Now, you're the man of the family. Your old father is tired. You know how difficult it is without your mother. My fellow-traveller has stopped along the route. Or perhaps she arrived at our peculiar destination more quickly than me. It's probably easier for believers. I don't have any regrets, but I can tell you that sometimes it's odd to think that each step, each second of our lives serves only one purpose. Whatever route you take, the last stop is the same for all of us. I don't like thinking about all that, but what can I do about it? You have to face the facts. Some days it all seems like a joke. You struggle over things, worry about them, get angry and one fine day, bingo, you lie down and it's all over. Do you remember when you were little you sometimes came home from school crying because one of the bigger boys had hit you, and your mother would stroke your head and say, 'It's nothing, darling.' You got on your high horse and shouted, 'No, it's not nothing, it's very serious!' It used to make her smile, she'd sing you a song, and you'd go to sleep. With us, it's the same. I mean, once you're an adult, you cry and stamp your feet and suffer, you tell yourself life's not fair and that you're dogged with bad luck, except that there's no one there to say, 'It's nothing, little one.' Sometimes, when I'm in a good mood, I imagine that that's what death is. A big hand which picks you up and sends you to sleep for ever trying to persuade you that it's not that bad.

Some legacy I'm leaving you! I've done my best to bring you both up. I can't say that I've taught you everything that I know because, in amongst it all, there were quite a lot of odds and ends that wouldn't have been any use to you. And I was never sure that I had anything to teach. I didn't spend long at school, and you so quickly came to understand for yourselves what I understood of life, much more quickly than me. I'm always lagging behind. My darling children, you both live in countries that I've only seen in photographs. I've never crossed the vast oceans that separate us, and who knows whether I ever will. You grew up in the new world, a world where people know everything. You are so much more intelligent than us. I could barely understand what you were talking about when you explained your new job to me. I know about computers; I've even used the Minitel at the Post Office. But 'programmer', what does that mean? You're designing the pattern, in a way. You see what I'm like? I refer everything back to me, to the few things that I know. Mind you, I've realised recently that the rag trade taught me a great deal. You know that I never chose that line of work. I accepted it by default. What I wanted to do was drive trains. Come to think of it, what sort of idea was that! Your mother practically turned green every time she had to set foot in a train. I must have driven her up the wall! You wouldn't believe it. Mind you, when it came to annoying others, she wasn't last in the queue. Always criticising, picking fault, a real rabbi's daughter. That's what it's like sharing your life with someone. Irritating each other in every possible way.

By the way, while we're on the subject, I know it's none of my business, but are you still seeing your girlfriend? What was her name? Carla, I think. Send me a picture some time. You know I've always liked pretty women. And, believe it or not, I still think about her because of that story you told me a while ago. Her three-year-old who ran away from home. Well, that's dressing it up a bit, but I seem to remember you found him on the doorstep because he wanted to go and live on his own in a tent. I don't know why I like that anecdote so much. Send me a picture of the little boy, too.

No, that's going too far. I've become very indiscreet in my old age. I'm like the pharaohs, gathering treasures to take them with me to my grave.

Look after yourself, my boy.

Your old father.

Max felt appeased. He felt, as he so rarely had before, the very particular brand of pleasure that comes from doing one's duty. Perhaps that was what had been eating at him recently. You didn't bring children into the world just to sit and watch them grow. You had to take care of them, watch over them. Basile was forty-six. Forty-six! Half a lifetime, and yet he was still a young man.

By the time he was his age, Max had started going grey, he had aches in his knees and he would sometimes wake up more tired than when he went to bed. And he had had two children. What on earth had Basile got up to in all these years? The enigma of his son's far-away life. He had passed exams, done courses, applied for jobs. He had probably met women. He was beautiful like his mother, long-legged and aristocratic-looking with piercing, secretive black eyes. Why hadn't he had any children? Max wondered.

When he himself had been a young man, girls never stopped getting pregnant; you almost hesitated to kiss them. Every woman was a belly, fertile in spite of herself. Life was an accident. It was a nuisance but at least you ran a chance of being surprised and overtaken by events. Birth control was quite something. Which man or woman could confirm in all conscience that he or she actually wanted a child? What would you do with it? Is the world all that beautiful? How would you bring it up? What sort of idiot would decide to become, say, a gardener just like that? You have to have the know-how for that as for everything else. Who then could consider themselves up to cultivating flowers that are so much more dangerous and vulnerable than any other? Max suddenly felt as if someone had taken the joker out of a pack of cards. What was the point in going on if chance had been taken out of the game?

Now I've started thinking about things, the old man realised in astonishment. He resented it almost immediately. He wasn't equipped to think. His mind was clogged with contradictions, saturated with knots. A reactionary idiot. The hour would soon strike and he would only get what he deserved. Who was he to judge progress in the world and the advances made by science? He would have been the first to put his head in his hands if his daughter had come home crying because she had had an 'accident'. He remembered young women destroyed by the shame, and those who had not survived the knitting needle, and the little bloody packages thrown into the river.

Basile didn't have any children, but he might still have a woman and someone else's child. He would go and see them. He would get Carla's son to call him grandpa. He would do anything for some continuity. Half a life is time enough to start a life again. Basile had all the time in the world.

On his way to an appointment at the bank, he decided to go into the travel agents.

The window was papered with special offers. The destinations were written out and then the prices in big colourful numbers. New York 1990F; Dublin 790F; Pisa 1450F. The United States is much further than Italy, Max thought, scratching his chin. Why only five hundred francs difference?

'Good morning,' he said and leant against the counter while he waited for the young woman to stop clattering on her computer keyboard.

'Can I help you?' she said, lazily looking up at him with big blue eyes framed by the ridiculous suntan mark left by her ski-glasses.

'I'd like to go to La Paz, please.'

'Sorry, where was that?'

'In Bolivia. It still is, I think.'

The young woman burst out laughing.

'I was afraid I hadn't heard correctly,' she said. 'La Paz in Bolivia, then?'

She opened a catalogue and started leafing through it.

'Yes, Bolivia,' said Max, irritated by the half smile that lingered on the young woman's chapped lips.

'Thank you,' she said. 'I'm looking for the company. Let's see.'

She went back to clattering on the computer.

'I can offer you a rate of 5,655F inclusive of taxes with a stop-off in Buenos Aires. When would you like to leave?'

'In June, round about the fifteenth.'

'Yes, that's fine. And what about the return journey?'

There won't be any return journey, thought Max. He hesitated for a moment.

'How long would you like to stay?' asked the young woman with a sigh.

'In fact, what I'd like to do is to go on to Tokyo.'

'In Japan?'

'Precisely.'

'So I'll book you a return flight Paris/La Paz/Paris, and then the same thing for Tokyo.'

'Do I have to come back by Paris?'

The young woman explained that if he didn't come back by Paris he would have to order tickets from several different airlines, one-way flights in business class, which cost a bomb, and the transfers would take for ever, and that she didn't think it was very sensible. Max was crushed. He knew that travelling wasn't easy, but he didn't know it was this bad! He asked her to look up the prices all the same. He would think about it.

'That puts the whole trip at about . . . Now, I don't want to get this wrong. Seventy thousand francs,' she said, separating out each syllable and with her eyes popping out of her head.

'Very good,' said Max, taking the piece of paper that she was holding out to him.

At least he would have a good reason to go to the bank.

'And I thought I was late!' cried Max as he went into Nina Brodsky's little apartment.

'Oh, there's no set time,' replied the old woman slyly.

'I think I must be the first to arrive.'

The corridor, whose walls were adorned with display cabinets cluttered with curios, led to a square sitting-room lit by a bay window. A large light with crystal pendants hung from the ceiling. On the two armchairs and on the matching sofa (velvet in a beautiful English green) cotton lace antimacassars indicated where you should rest your head. Mrs Brodsky offered Max a seat and she in turn sat down facing him, perched on half a buttock with her knees elegantly crossed and bent back underneath her. As she was very small, the antimacassar created a sort of halo for her, like a head of curlers, and it made Max smile.

'It's not a palace,' she said, 'but it's very functional, with everything you need within reach.'

Max looked around him at the wallpaper with its beige leafy design, the Vallauris porcelain fruit bowl which had pride of place on the cherry-wood table, and the Persian-style rug with red and gold rosette motifs. It was all admirably well maintained and impeccably clean.

'Can I offer you something to drink?' asked Nina. 'I've made some *oumentashen** for you.'

'It's not that time of year,' said Max.

'There's no particular time of year for cakes,' retorted Mrs

---

* Literally 'Haman pockets'. Central European cakes made for the Jewish holiday of *Purim*

Brodsky getting to her feet quickly. 'Don't move. I'm just disappearing into the kitchen for a minute to make the tea.'

'Tea, what a good idea!' said Max.

He'd had half a litre of the stuff before leaving his apartment and was wondering how he could consume another drop of it.

Once she had left the room, he took the liberty of looking at each detail at his leisure. The self-lined curtains with their elaborate tiebacks, the pictures on the walls (a sea view, a Pierrot whose costume was livened up with sequins, a montage of photographs which single-handedly represented all the stages of life from babyhood to old age passing through awkward adolescence and smiling maturity.) Max was in familiar territory. Most of his friends had dreamed of this sort of cosy nest; Telma had too, probably, but his wife had never achieved this degree of coherence.

Was it because of him and his endless 'clutter'? Or even because of her, her resistance, her spirit of destruction? She called it her *dibbuk*. It was a demon that inhabited her, an irresistible force with a will of its own. Max envisaged this imaginary gnome armed with a club. It would sleep for hours on end and then would wake suddenly and wield its weapon, smashing anything it didn't like.

It's nine o'clock in the evening, the children are asleep breathing peacefully under their covers, the kitchen is tidy, the bills paid, a smile is spreading over Telma's beautiful, angular face and suddenly, bang! Dibbuk wakes up, he gives a great blow of his club right in the middle of the sitting-room. Her smile disappears, she knits her brows and wrings her hands. 'What's the matter, my darling? Are you feeling all right?' No reply emerges from her tightly sealed lips. The appalling temptation: to succumb to the peace and satisfaction of domestic happiness. Telma gets up to drink a glass of water. As she rinses it out, she breaks it;

as she picks up the pieces, she cuts herself; this is the price she has to pay to get to sleep.

The curtains in the children's bedroom didn't have a hem, because on the evening that Telma started to stitch it up, Basile had coughed and then been sick. She had bathed and comforted her baby, hung the over-long curtains and given up. Their plates were all mismatched because half of them had been broken. Those that were left were chipped and if Max, in an unforgivable momentary lapse of concentration, offered to replace the lot – 'let's have a look round the shopping centre, I've had a really good bonus' – it was a crime, there was screaming and shouting, *Oï gevald*, Telma would get into a complete state. It was not open to discussion. Max should have guessed as much. This was exactly what he had loved about Telma, her unfailing loyalty, her incredible memory. How petty Mrs Brodsky's satisfactions seemed to him now, each thing in its proper place, and the magic feather duster which sweeps away the ash along with the dust. Some of the balls of fluff under the furniture were probably more valuable in Telma's eyes than their most precious ornaments.

'A nice scalding hot cup of tea,' exclaimed Nina from the doorway, her arms weighed down with a tray.

'Let me help you,' said Max getting to his feet.

'No, please,' she said reproachfully. 'You're my guest.'

On the subject of guests, hadn't Mrs Brodsky mentioned a gathering of friends, a little party for the members of the club? There were only two glasses next to the teapot.

'Shouldn't we wait for the others?' Max asked, mercilessly.

Nina blushed and raised her eyes to heaven. Her artless subterfuge had been discovered. She sat down at the table and served the tea.

'You've refused my invitations three times,' she explained. 'I wasn't going to go so far as to beg you. I thought that if there were several of us, you would accept more readily. And then, at the last minute, I didn't invite the others.'

The naïvety of the lie made Max smile. He had fallen into the trap. There was no point in making a song and dance about it.

'Here,' she said, offering him the plate of cakes, 'help yourself, they're lovely and fresh.'

Max took the little crescent shape of shortcrust pastry and turned it over in his hand. It was impressively regular, perfectly golden and slightly darker round the edges. Telma's biscuits always looked as if they'd come out of a dustbin. Her strudels exploded in the oven and the apple purée leaked out, her short-cakes were never completely round, her cheesecakes would fluff up on one side and stay flat on the other, and as for her *oumen-tashen*, they looked more like scrunched up balls of paper than little pasties. But they were delicious and they melted in the mouth, having taken hours of preparation with the tips of little fingers, each one cut out and stained with juice from beetroots or walnut shells. He bit into the biscuit, amazed at how sweet this posthumous culinary adultery felt. Nina was watching him out of the corner of her eye, a temptress with a wrinkled face and faltering smile. She's like me, he told himself. A nice little egotist who's done rather well for herself. He knew, as he tasted the biscuit, that she was one of the ingenuous few who, torn between guilt and *joie de vivre*, quietly make their way to an infinitely more cosy grave than most.

'Delicious,' said Max.

Nina smiled and bit delicately into one of her perfect little cakes.

'I've always enjoyed entertaining,' she said. 'I've got three grandchildren, and I've been a great-grandmother for six months. How about you?'

'I . . .' Max began.

He hesitated for a moment. He wasn't used to this sort of small talk. Women's talk, as far as he was concerned.

'You don't have to tell me,' said Nina. 'Everyone has a right to their little bit of mystery. My husband spoke very little. He thought I was too talkative. Even when we were playing cards, he would scold me: "We're not playing chatterbox".'

A wise man amongst wise men. Max suddenly felt a surge of pity for this departed husband who had had to put up with this woman. Perhaps she had killed him with the force of her chitter and the strength of her chatter, gently disembowelling him with the butter-knife of her excruciating conversation.

'The problem is,' she continued, 'because I'm deaf, I don't realise I'm doing it. I talk and talk, otherwise I just have the buzzing in my head. A great fly shut in up there driving me half mad.'

'You're deaf?' Max repeated, surprised by this unexpected lack of guile.

'Why not? Because I answer when you speak? I can lip-read, and anyway most of the time I know more or less what people are going to say before they even open their mouths. It's not telepathy. It's just what old age does for you. My eardrums were damaged by a bomb blast. Torn, I think. My older sister and I were lying down in the grass with our hands on our heads. We'd been running and suddenly my sister said: "Put your hands on your head." She threw herself to the ground and I copied her. There was a great noise which went right through my head. Do you know that magic trick where the scarf goes in one ear and comes out of the other? I've always loved that one. The bomb did the same thing. It went in on one side, dug a big tunnel and came out on the other side. I never saw my sister again. She was thrown into the air. I didn't want to see where she fell. I just set off walking dead ahead of me. From then on I only met the kindest of people.'

She smiled and offered the plate of biscuits to Max again. He declined with a shake of the head.

'Luckily, my husband had very good hearing. When the children were babies he was always the one who woke in the night. He would give me a little nudge with his elbow and I'd know it was time for their feed. What's strange, you see, is that it's never really bothered me. I can sing as well as the next person, I can sing lullabies in three different languages. The ENT specialist told me that I could still gauge the pitch of a sound.'

The trap was deeper than Max had anticipated. He didn't dare say a word. Without wishing to boast, he thought he was fairly unpredictable, and he was afraid that the slapdash way in which he articulated his words wouldn't allow his hostess to understand him. He drank a mouthful of scalding tea. Just to win some time, he got up to look at the paintings on the walls.

'I painted that one in '56,' said Nina, indicating the sea view, 'I'm particularly fond of it because we were up in the mountains when I thought of it. My husband loved walking. But I start tripping up after just three paces. He took the eldest two with him, and I stayed in the chalet with Lolek, our youngest. A sweetheart. I could give him a bit of bread dough and he would play at my feet all afternoon.'

'Are you a painter?' Max asked very loudly, articulating exaggeratedly.

'Painter would be going a bit far. I've always been lucky. I married an American just after the war. His family had emigrated at the beginning of the century. He'd spent all of his childhood in New York but, strangely enough, he'd never got over actually arriving there. The part that he had really enjoyed was the boat journey. When you know what sort of conditions they travelled in, you ask yourself how it's possible. Charles was a one-off. Look at his name for a start, Charles, do you think that's a normal

name? I think his mother was a bit cuckoo. He was in one of
the first wave of parachute landings. He wasn't a very warry type.
I think he only joined up to come back to Europe. His strength
was for business affairs. I never had to work, but I don't like
having nothing to do, so I turned my hand to painting. I took
drawing classes. I even gave some. I was quite a good teacher,
specially with children.'

Max prepared himself to speak. He wanted to tell Mrs Brodsky
how surprised he was to hear this, to share the incredible coinci-
dence with her. But he couldn't see how to condense his story
into a simple sentence. Talking to the deaf makes you dumb, he
told himself.

'It's beautifully done.'

'Are you interested in art?' she asked. 'I did the Pierrot in '70.
It was commissioned by the woman who lived across the landing
from us. When she died her daughter gave it back to me. People
are funny, aren't they? But I couldn't very well throw it away.
Mrs Fritz . . . that was her name – can you believe it? – Mrs Fritz
was very kind to me. She must have weighed well over fifteen
stone, and she was only about five foot three, she had a very
husky deep voice and she always sounded out of breath. She
reminded me of a boxer. Well, an old boxer, a retired sportsman.
Do you see what I mean?'

Max wasn't really sure but he nodded.

'It wouldn't have been right to have thrown the painting away
or to have put it in a cupboard. Especially as her daughter . . .
well, I suppose it's normal. It must be difficult being the daughter
of a very fat woman.'

This time Max raised an eyebrow as a sign of interrogation.

'A girl likes to be proud of her mother,' Nina explained. 'She
wants to be like her, it's natural. When the mother is very fat or
very ugly – but nowadays fat is worse than ugly – it's as if she

were saying to her daughter: either you love me and you grow up like me, or you grow up different which means you don't love me. It's difficult to cope with. Do you understand?'

Max wasn't concentrating. He wasn't expecting to be involved.

'You say that because you yourself are thin,' he said.

'You're absolutely right,' Nina Brodsky replied straight away. 'I don't think before I speak, that's my problem. Besides, my eldest daughter is on the plump side and I've never thought that she loved me any less than the younger one.'

She chuckled and flushed slightly.

'I'm going to be honest with you, Mr Opass.'

Max paled.

'I know everything that's going on. I didn't want to say anything to you but I realize that it's ridiculous. I've never been able to lie. I'm not actually this talkative normally. It's just there's something I keep sidestepping.'

Max wondered whether she had mistaken him for someone else. He had nothing to hide, nothing to be ashamed of, but he was on his guard all the same, afraid that some distant scrap of his past was going to rise up before him, and ready to answer for himself if he were accused of anything.

'I think that I can help you. It must seem strange to you, but I'm convinced that I'm the only person who really understands what you're looking for. I've got it in me. I just have to express it. The others will let you down. Don't think I'm trying to do away with the competition. Above all, I want to persuade you to trust in me.'

'My dear Mrs Brodsky,' Max said, getting to his feet. 'I'm sure that you're very gifted and I don't doubt that you can work miracles, but I don't need anyone. I think you're making a mistake.'

A clairvoyant, that was all he needed. He had come across

several in the course of his life. This one didn't look the type, she was short of a scarf and a few jangling bangles. Crafty to disguise herself as an upright old lady. Where was she hiding her crystal ball? When he was little a fortune-teller had foretold that his mother would have numerous descendants spread all over the world. She probably spent more time reading newspapers than the lines on people's hands, but he had to acknowledge that she had not been wrong.

'Show me the photographs! Please!' cried Nina.

Max let himself slump back into the chair, aghast.

'I'm so sorry,' she went on. 'I should have mentioned it straight away, but how could I? I'm shy, despite what you might think. It's Jacques who put me on the trail. Mr Jacques, the bookseller, do you know him? He did the enlargements for you with his machine. It's a small world, you know.'

'What's that oddball gone and told you?'

'You may well call him an oddball but when you've been a widow for ten years you take what consolations you can. He might come across as a bit abrupt, but he's a very generous man.'

Without being able to explain why, Max felt a little pang of jealousy. He had imagined that Mrs Brodsky was interested in him. He had quite made up his mind not to respond to her advances, but he had taken pleasure in evoking a vague romance.

'Jacques and I tell each other everything. I mentioned you to him, because of the scene you made at the club, do you remember? And one evening as he came in he told me about the photos. From then on I made my enquiries. Everyone knows everyone round here. When you know how to go about it, news reaches you fast. Without bragging, I'd say I could have had a good career as a spy.'

'In the police force is more like it,' Max said between his teeth.

'Sorry?'

'I said you would have done very well in the police force,' he said out loud.

'The police? How awful, that's nothing like as smart! I prefer to use my talents to serve art.'

'I've given away everything I had,' said Max.

'What do you mean?'

'The originals are with Angus, the slides with Mrs Lazieu and the photocopies with the two youngsters. I haven't got anything left.'

'And the negatives? You must have the negatives somewhere?' Nina asked inquisitively.

'I put them in the safe,' Max replied.

'And you've swallowed the key, is that it?'

Max started to laugh.

'You're a strange creature, Mrs Brodsky.'

'I'll take that as a compliment, if I may.'

'In the circumstances . . .'

When it came down to it, there were still plenty of surprises. In her own way, Mrs Brodsky was quite something. It was she who had come looking for him.

'We'll do a deal, if you want,' he continued. 'You tell me everything you know about it, and then I'll tell you the story right from the beginning.'

'I don't know anything,' Nina replied tartly.

'Come on. Five minutes ago you were telling me it's a small world. From what you were saying you were the Mata Hari of the Thirteenth Arrondissement.'

'I don't trust you,' she admitted. 'I know how this will end. I'll tell you what I know and then you'll leave. Right now, I've got you. And I'm not ready to let you go. Have another cake.'

'They're not poisoned, I hope?'

'You'll know that later, too. For now, my lips are sealed, the deaf can play dumb.'

Max obediently bit into another cake, his taste buds aroused. He had never tasted anything better.

'I don't know how I manage it,' he said with his mouth full. 'Women always lay down the law with me.'

'Really?'

Max nodded his head and took a third *oumentash*. Tea gives you an appetite, he said to himself.

'I attract them, you know? I may not look like it now but, in my time, I was a hell of a . . .'

'A hell of a lady-killer?' suggested Nina.

'Well, yes, let's call it that. They fell like flies, but as soon as they'd fallen they got up again. Do you know the story of Doctor Jekyll? All sweetness and light and then from one minute to the next, complete monsters. I swear to you.'

'I believe you.'

'Look at you, for example. I didn't watch my back. I said "yes, miss" like a schoolboy for the register. You come across as the weak type. Don't take that the wrong way, that's the second compliment I've paid you.'

She pulled a face.

'Without prying, can I ask how old you are, Mrs Brodsky? It's no longer rude once you get beyond seventy, is it?'

'Seventy-six last month,' she replied proudly. 'Believe it or not, I've never been afraid of growing old. And, if you want to know everything, I don't think I'm at all bad for my age.'

Max was enchanted by her little air of defiance.

'Out of the mouths of the elderly comes the truth,' he said.

'Elderly yourself. I bet you're at least eighty.'

'Ah-ha, you've got me there, but I'm not going under yet. It just happens that I've never been afraid of growing old either. In fact, the older I get the more I realise that that's a pretty ugly word to describe what's happening to us. When I was a young man I thought that the old were as decrepit on the inside as they are on the outside. Apparently, once we reach twenty all our cells, with no exceptions, start disintegrating at alarming speed. If that were true, you and I wouldn't be able to speak as we are. Do you see what I mean?'

'Absolutely.'

Max was relieved at last to find someone he could talk to who understood him.

'I'm not in my first flush of youth any longer, I'll grant you. But, recently, I've felt ... how can I put this? You're going to make fun of me but never mind. I've felt as if I'm having a growth spurt. I'm growing a couple of inches every minute.'

He was perfectly aware of the ambiguous nature of what he had said and he revelled in the effect it had on his hostess. She was literally hanging on his every word, leaning slightly towards him with her hands crossed over her bony knees.

'I'm gaining in amplitude,' he went on. 'Do you know "The Albatross"?'

'Sorry?'

'It's a poem by ... what's his name again? A classic. His name escapes me. Never mind. Suffice it to say, my mind is still expanding.'

'You see, my dear friend, I'm not laughing,' said Nina. 'I would never have thought – I'm terribly sorry if this upsets you – no, really, I would never have thought that you were so refined. May I tell you an anecdote?'

'You don't know how to hold your tongue, or your promises for that matter. I thought it was my turn to talk.'

'Promises don't mean anything any more at our age. By the

time you've kept them, you might be dead. Better to break them as soon as possible. What do you think?'

She laughed with a very flirtatious sideways glance, and carried on.

'Last year Jacques and I went on a holiday together. A week on the shores of Lake Como in Italy. It's a beautiful place. With quite exceptional views. The air was so pure that I felt I was getting younger with every breath I took. We were whiling away the end of an afternoon in deck chairs, Jacques was reading *Gazzetta dello Sport*, a pink rag which talks about practically nothing but football. I was watching the sun gradually turning red. When I was little my mother used to say that you should never look straight at the sun, it made you blind. She also used to say: "Don't pull faces, if the wind changes you'll stay like that." I told my children a fair amount of nonsense myself. But we're not here to talk about my mother, poor thing.'

Nina wrinkled her nose and rubbed her hands together, palm to palm like a fly preparing to fly off.

'So there I was watching the sun, one evening, and two mosquitoes came and flew around above my head. They were dancing round in circles, chasing each other I think. I looked up and I said to myself: "Look, my soul and my conscience are dancing around above my head." One of the mosquitoes disappeared suddenly and I thought: "My conscience has left, that only leaves my soul." I had a feeling of peace that we probably only experience a handful of times in a lifetime. A wonderful feeling of letting go.'

She sighed, unfolded her short slim legs and held them out horizontally for a moment, which made her look very girlish.

'I see what you mean with your story about the bird. Little by little we shed everything that we've learned, only our souls are left, and they start to spread and spread to infinity.'

124

Nina Brodsky stopped talking. Her gaze, which had been lost in the design of the wallpaper, came back to lock onto Max's eyes. The pale green of her irises was shiny and transparent. Her drooping eyelids were traced with a thousand and one pathways. Max felt uncomfortable. His heart was beating slowly. He felt as if, with each breath he inhaled, the padded drumstick of a kettle drum was beating deep in his chest. He was too hot. He had pins and needles between his ankles and his knees. His palms were clammy and his forehead damp.

'But you were talking about women,' she went on, her voice slightly husky and unsure of itself. 'It's a good subject.'

What's happening to me? Max wondered. He felt shaky. What had she put in the biscuits? Every mouthful made him more talkative. She was watching him sweetly. Without another word, she held out the plate to him. He took a fourth *oumentash* and started talking.

'I haven't known that many women, you know. But I've got my own little theory about that.'

Having swallowed the cake in one mouthful he continued.

'They're angry. All of them. And I don't know why. They resent us. They either make us pay for it by reducing us to slavery, or they sink into unhappiness and cry from morning till night. When all's said and done, I think I prefer the first version.'

Nina Brodsky raised her eyes heavenwards, looking doubtful.

'Telma was between the two.'

Nina's face lit up. She was onto her prey at last.

Max realised immediately and smiled at her.

'You're inquisitive, aren't you?'

'Very. Ever since I was tiny. It's like an illness.'

'Telma was my wife. It was her portrait that I wanted to have painted. She died a year ago. A year and two months exactly. I didn't say any prayers for the *yahrzeit*.* I only know the first three words of the kaddish. But I did stop shaving and I made this decision: I've met three artists, and I've commissioned each of them.'

'Three? Why three? Wasn't one enough for you?'

Max hadn't really thought about this. There could have been fifteen of them.

'By chance,' he replied, a little embarrassed. 'One thing led to another. I told myself I was more likely to get a good painting if I asked several people to do them. The law of averages, really.'

'What wouldn't we do to amuse ourselves? It's true isn't it, Max?'

'That's got nothing to do with it, Nina. That is your name, isn't it? I play bridge as a way of amusing myself. You should know that well enough.'

'Bridge? Who's talking about that? I'm talking about a different kind of amusement, and you know full well.'

Max scratched his beard. Did he know? After his brief flash of conscience, his mind had closed shut like an oyster.

Nina stood up, moved her chair closer to the sofa that her guest was sitting on and sat back down less than a metre from him. Without looking at him, she put her bony hand with its well-tended nails onto Max's right knee.

'It's not easy for anyone,' she said quietly. 'Old age weaves tighter and tighter clothes for us. You put it very well, we go on growing, but only on the inside, and who can tell? Who cares? We have to accept that we're rotting on our own two feet. But I refuse to, you see. So long as I'm getting older that's a good sign. It means that I'm not dead and that's a lot to be getting on with.'

---

* Yiddish name for the anniversary of the death of a loved one for whom there is compulsory mourning.

They stayed like that for a long time, without speaking or moving, while the sun charted its way across the walls and eventually disappeared behind a red-brick building that rose up from the pavement opposite.

'Stay to supper,' Nina ordered in a voice that had been deadened by too long a silence.

'You see, that's exactly what I was saying. Reduced to slavery.'

Max got up and laid the table while Mrs Brodsky busied herself in front of her oven.

When he had finished setting out the cutlery he sat down, ravaged by an inexplicable appetite. He watched his hostess surreptitiously. She was small with tiny joints that looked as if they could be broken with one hand. Her straight woollen skirt was knee-length, a classic length, Max told himself, perfect elegance. Her movements were precise and measured. Having chopped a large onion, she slid it into a sizzling pan, and Max felt himself succumbing. She turned to look at him as she turned over the pieces of chicken that she was browning. Her little round face, framed by her urchin-style white hair, had two dimples just below her cheekbones which were high and tremendously pronounced.

'It's just left-overs,' she said. 'I didn't know you'd be . . .'

A professional liar, thought Max replying with a smile that pretended credulity.

Nina Brodsky not only made excellent cakes, she was a genius in the kitchen. The meat was tender and deliciously fragrant, the kacha was the perfect consistency, and the accompanying stock – which, she had pointed out, was impeccably clear – had an incomparably delicate flavour. They clinked their glasses of vodka and after two glasses Nina started telling Max nonsense stories that had him bent double with laughter.

Max felt light-hearted. Night had fallen and, for the first time in ages, he felt completely relaxed. For dessert, they each had half a melon, and it was so sweet that they couldn't help themselves rapturously commenting on it, their hands joined together and their eyes to the heavens.

'So, these photographs?' Nina asked again, when she had cleared the table.

'Stubborn as a mule!' said Max.

'I have every vice,' she replied, taking his arm. 'Come, we'll be more comfortable in the sitting-room.'

They sat down side by side on the sofa. Their faces were lit by just one lamp on a small table.

'Be nice, Max,' she insisted. 'I'm sure that you've got them on you now, somewhere.'

She started searching him, patting his jacket like a mischievous little girl. Max sat rigidly in his seat.

'I surrender, *Herr General*,' he exclaimed, pulling from his inside pocket an envelope which he waved under his hostess's nose like a white flag.

Nina seized it and opened it carefully.

'Now, let's see,' she said. 'Bother! I haven't got my glasses.'

Max handed her his and she put them on her delicate nose.

'How do I look?' she asked, looking at him over the top of the lenses that were far too big for her narrow face.

'Just right,' said Max.

'Third compliment?'

'Don't let's exaggerate anything,' he replied, sobering suddenly.

Telma had come out of the envelope. Oh, the bad genie was out! It really was no laughing matter. She was watching him from her new observation post. Flirting with a widow. Aren't you ashamed? And what a widow! Double infidelity: to the memory of her husband and to her current lover. All they needed now was for Mr Jacques to turn up unexpectedly and the vaudeville scene would be complete.

Nina Brodsky looked quickly through the photographs. She was irritated.

'They're all the same!'

'What do you mean?'

'Well, look, three of this one, four of that one.'

She handed him his glasses so that he could see for himself, put he brushed them aside.

'I know the pictures, thank you. I made several copies just in case.'

He suddenly felt contemptible. The supper that had followed hard on the heels of the tea weighed down on his stomach.

'So there are actually only five of them,' said Nina, resealing the envelope.

Max shrugged his shoulders.

'That'll be enough,' she added in a more conciliatory tone. 'They're not very good, but they'll do. Don't worry about it.'

'I haven't asked you for anything,' murmured Max. What was the point of fighting?

He sank back against the back of the chair. His eyelids were burning, his throat tight. What had he hoped he would gain by asking for so many versions, to set up some sort of routine? Nina had pinpointed his problem precisely: he needed ways of amusing himself. Without admitting it to himself he had pictured himself travelling all over town, then all over the country, even the whole world, looking for the ideal person to execute the task, the perfect portrait artist. It was a new interpretation of the railway for him. The Railwayman would not only have to drive the train but to lay the tracks as he went along. Max was exhausted. He thought of the big consoling hand that he had evoked in his letter to Basile, and he felt that he was ready to meet it. It could pick him up, right here, the very next minute. Well, actually, no. That wouldn't be right. He couldn't die in Nina Brodsky's apartment.

Nadya wouldn't appreciate it. He sat up again, having made up his mind to leave.

'Can I keep them?' asked Nina.

'But what are you going to do with them?'

'What do you think? Black magic perhaps? I want to do something for you. If you want to have a portrait of your wife, you shall have one.'

Max let his head fall into his hands. A stifled sob racked his chest. He felt lost. This whole business was ridiculous. What an idea! He would have to put a stop to it all. Max didn't want to hear another word on the subject. He looked at the envelope in Nina's hands. Make it disappear, let the paper dissolve and the colours fade. He wouldn't survive another portrait.

Faces spun round in his mind, the carousel of his painters. Angus, a little bull with the hands of a princess; Diane, an elegant swan with a head made of parchment; Virginie, a gorgon with three children's faces, her smooth forehead framed by the more rounded foreheads of her sleeping children; Frédéric, a gentle fawn with eyes like Bambi; Marion, a filly foal with a thick mane; and, joining them as they chased round in endless circles, Nina, a white cat with flour on her paws. What did it all mean?

He felt a cool hand on the nape of his neck.

'Have a sleep, Max,' Nina murmured. 'Lie down. I'll get you a blanket. You can sleep here if you like. It's late. I wouldn't feel happy letting you leave in this state.'

Max complied and, having taken off his jacket, he rested his head on the cushions that she had put at the end of the sofa.

'Let me do it,' she whispered. 'I'll take your shoes off.'

He didn't have an ounce of strength left in him. What little energy he had left was totally focused on the exhausting process of damming his tears. Lying flat out with his eyes closed, his fists clenched and his knees trembling, he tried to fight off the battalions of questions assailing him.

Nina, kneeling next to him, no longer dared to touch him.

'When my husband died,' she started in a shaky voice, 'No, first I'll have to explain. He left very suddenly. I wasn't expecting it. There are always heaps of consoling words to make mourning easier. If the person has been ill, then you've had time to get used to the idea. If the person was old, you have to be grateful that they got that far. Charles was still young. He was sixty five and – perhaps it was because I loved him – I didn't think he was any more wrinkled than he had been at forty. He was a calm, abstemious man. He didn't smoke, didn't drink. One evening, he went to sleep as usual. He said: "Sweet dreams, my darling." Dreams were a real hobby of his. If he forgot to say: "Sweet dreams" or if I forgot to say: "You too, my darling", he tossed about in bed all night, unable to get a wink of sleep.

'When he woke up, the first thing he did was to tell me about his dreams. Then I would tell him mine. But, most of the time, I couldn't remember anything of the images I had seen in the night. I'd open my eyes and my mind would be blank. So I'd invent things. As the years went by I built myself a sort of system. There were animals, birds, a few insects and very occasionally wild cats; there were places too, some that were very familiar and others that I'd only seen in photographs; as for the characters, I'd use the family and, sometimes, strangers that I couldn't identify. I was careful to keep changing the length of the dreams and the amount of detail. I even said that I couldn't remember anything about four or five times a month. Then we could get up and start the day. But on that particular evening he went to sleep, quite peacefully, I said: "sweet dreams", and when I woke up he was no longer breathing. I realised straight away. The silence . . .'

A great sob prevented her from speaking for a moment.

'He was lying there, next to me, on his back with his mouth slightly open. I didn't dare move. I wanted to go back to sleep. I tried to convince myself that it was just a nightmare. I closed my eyes, my heart was so heavy that I found it difficult to breathe. I said his name. Several times. Then I started to cry. The stupid thing is – I can tell you this, I know you'll understand – I wasn't crying because he was dead. I was crying because, for once, I'd had a dream, a really lovely dream. I'd spent the whole night gliding over endless hills, woods and lakes. Every now and again I'd land on a church steeple or on a farmhouse roof and I'd been able to sense every thought of the people and the animals. An incredible bombardment of sound. Babel. But I understood everything. My mind was like a set of keys, I could open each lock and hear so clearly, more clearly than I'd been able to for forty years. I woke up smiling, cured.

'I sat there in bed and talked to myself. I told my dream in tears. I asked Charles to forgive me for all those years of lying, all the dreams I'd fabricated. Nothing can prepare us for death. But then nothing can prepare us for life, either. There's no apprenticeship. When it all comes down to it, you're no better off than a sheep or a cockroach. It comes, and it goes, we don't know why and we can't do anything about it.

'When my children were little, they would sometimes ask me whether I or their father would die. Children think about death a lot. I would say: "No, only people who are very old or very ill die." I'd explain that life was long and it only ended when it was all finished. I was so persuasive that I convinced myself, at the time I thought that it was simple and fair. As time goes by, you get closer to death. But sometimes that's not true. It's not like that, and, if you think about it a bit, you realise that the distance between us and death has got nothing to do with how much time has passed, some people die when they're six months old, others when they're five years old and some are still on their feet when they're ninety-eight. None of it makes any sense, don't you think?'

'You're not a person when you're six months old.'

'To yourself, perhaps not, but to others, yes, completely.'

Max didn't like this sort of conversation. Talking about it didn't change anything. He wanted to go to sleep. She could stay there, yes. He didn't like what she was saying, but feeling her presence, hearing the quiet rustling of the lining of her skirt, the sudden clinking of her rings against the wood of her chair, breathing in her perfume, which was sweet and fleeting like the smell of a garden rose, letting himself be lulled by her voice . . . But being wary, nonetheless, she'd sent her husband to sleep for ever, hadn't she?

When was he ever going to stop being afraid of women? They were no more sorcerers than he was with his gallery of painters.

'You will let me do the portrait, won't you?' Nina asked.

Max didn't answer.

'Are you asleep?'

'No, I'm trying to think.'

'Don't think. Say yes. It'll be the last one. Then you can . . .'

'I can die in peace.'

'That's not what I was thinking,' said Nina, embarrassed.

It wasn't very kind to exploit the situation like that. He knew exactly what he could then do, but he wouldn't tell her. One secret can drive out another.

Mathusalem

Nina had switched off the light and eclipsed herself on tiptoe. Max was not asleep. He had not dared to ask her to stay. His closed eyelids and peaceful breathing had deceived the old woman. Just as he had as a child, he had pretended to be asleep, withdrawing himself from the world, the better to spy on it. But the world was no longer the same. A desert stretched out to infinity, calm as a graveyard.

At thirteen, after a more than usually serious asthma attack, Max had been sent away to stay with a friend of his father's who had a farm on the banks of a river. He could no longer remember the name of the village, but he could see himself on the train, alone for the first time. In his smart town suit he thought he looked like a man, and he believed that the other passengers thought so too. A carriage was waiting for him at the station. A man he had never met had shaken his hand and asked him to climb into the back. The sun and the wind buffeted and parted the ripe corn into different hairstyles.

At the house he had been served some green soup and black bread. He had thanked them with a silent smile. The father and mother exchanged few words. The daughter, who was five years older than him, didn't look at him once. She ate delicately with lowered eyes. Although it was still broad daylight they had closed all the shutters. Max was exhausted by the journey, the summer, the silence, lost on the banks of a river whose name he had never been told.

The building was almost entirely given over to cowsheds. The parents slept in the kitchen. They put Max into a little room with no windows. The walls were made of loosely joined planks of wood which let in the intoxicating fragrance of the conifers, and white blades of light from the still blazing sun. As soon as he lay down, Max closed his eyes with a heavy head and a light heart.

A few minutes later the door opened; he didn't move. Tatiana came in; she came up to the bed on tiptoes and leant towards Max. He could feel her breath on his eyelashes. Whatever happens he mustn't blink, he must breathe gently.

Once she was sure that the child was asleep, she turned towards the wall and undressed. Max still didn't dare move. His left leg was beginning to feel stiff, but it was a price worth paying. He opened his eyes a fraction. What he then saw completed his paralysis. The dusty rays of sunlight cut Tatiana's body into slices of blue and lilac. The tips of her breast, which looked nearly black, pointed towards the door as she took off her blouse with her arms raised above her head. Her tummy, shimmering in a constellation of sequins, quivered as it was stroked by the evening air. When her long legs emerged from her petticoats like the limbs of a grasshopper Max couldn't help himself opening his eyes wide, but he then shut them immediately. His heart was beating so hard that for a moment he was worried that she would hear it. When she slipped into bed next to him, clutching her nightshirt to her, he opened one eyelid and glimpsed the dark down that bordered her navy blue lips.

Terrified, he went straight to sleep, as if he had been given a blow to the back of the neck. He was woken by screaming in the middle of the night. He sat bolt upright. The darkness was impenetrable. Tatiana was fighting with someone in her dream and her lungs were producing a formidable growl. The father

Mathusalem

came in and, without saying a word, took Max in his arms and put him on a straw bed next to an insomniac goat who was chewing noisily.

Over the next three weeks he never went back into the little windowless room. No one spoke a word. Max spent the rest of the stay talking to the animals and undertaking the rare tasks that he was asked – in kind and friendly tones – to complete by his hosts. When he returned home, the family doctor congratulated himself for the success of the treatment. His patient had been definitively cured.

What was he doing in Nina Brodsky's apartment? Half asleep, he could hear her drawing through the partition wall. A fine harvest he was going to have of this. He no longer felt the least glimmer of curiosity. She might just as well have served him up a Smiley face on a loose sheet of paper.

He had done his rounds the previous week. Each time he had been disappointed and relieved, feeling the sterile contentment of the Sphinx with its indecipherable enigma.

He had wandered round Paris with his pockets filled with wodges of bank notes. It was Virginie who had summoned him first.

'I'm not displeased with it,' she said on the telephone. 'I worked from the projected image. The results are pretty surprising, you'll see.'

Surprising, at least it had something going for it. The canvas was up on an easel and covered with a cloth. It was a Wednesday. Max had been greeted by the children's cries. The apartment was strewn with toys; dolls hung by their hair from the curtain strings, crooked towers of Lego made getting across the sitting-room into an obstacle course.

Garance looked like her mother with her thin square shoulders; she had two plaits coiled into a crown on top of her head.

Her eyebrows, which were extraordinarily mobile for her age, embroidered ten different expressions a minute. She went from great caution to ingratiating innocence and then amazement without losing a permanent air of anxiety, the slight crease that her mother had imprinted in the middle of her forehead, as if she had stamped her seal there.

'I couldn't get a child-minder,' Virginie had apologised as she opened the door.

Lies, always lies. Why not be honest? She had wanted to show her two most beautiful creations to her customer. It was actually fairly persuasive. The children had extravagant, round dark eyes with eyelashes that went on for ever. They were gentle and incredibly polite. They had held out their little hands in turn to shake the old man's hand.

'Pleased to meet you,' they had lisped.

Garance, the youngest and boldest, first; Paulo, half a head taller with his straight dark fringe covering his eyebrows, behind.

Virginie smiled, her cheeks pink.

'ONE! TWO! THREE!' announced Paulo who had climbed onto a chair.

The cloth flew off and unveiled the painting. A rectangular concoction some twenty by twenty-five centimetres. The paint had been applied with a spatula in big trails of beige, ochre and pink, underlined by darker areas that mimicked shadows, wrinkles and relief, and peppered here and there with brown patches which evoked rather too faithfully the complexion of the model in her mottled latter years. It was reminiscent of a *pâté campagnard*: meat re-heated in fat and coarsely chopped, a charming terrine of love.

'I started off with wax pastels,' said Virginie with a hesitant smile. 'And then I really went for it, oils.'

Telma's eyes, lost in this astonishingly carnal accumulation,

gleamed like those black glass buttons you sometimes find
stitched to the muzzles of teddy bears.

Max didn't know what to say.

'I projected the slides onto the wall,' Virginie explained, 'and
I did several sketches on tracing paper to make sure I got a good
likeness.'

Garance and Paulo framed their mother, proud and protective.
They were waiting for the old man's verdict.

Max moved closer to the easel and took the painting, looking
at it close up at first and then from further away, holding his
arm out horizontally.

'Be honest,' begged the young woman. 'Criticism is always
constructive.'

Max wasn't so sure.

'It's exactly what I wanted,' he said, trembling slightly.

Virginie raised her arms skywards, cheered on by her little
supporters.

'I knew I could do it!' she exclaimed. 'I knew I had it in me.
I'm so happy. You don't know what this means to me.'

Probably not, the old man thought. He didn't have the least idea.
The painting didn't look like anything to him, least of all Telma.

He took the envelope that he had prepared from his inside
pocket.

'Here,' he said, handing it to Virginie. 'You've certainly earned
it.'

The young woman took the money and stuffed into the drawer
of the sideboard.

'I won't disguise the fact that I put a lot of work into it,' she
said, running her hands over her face. 'Sometimes I'd work all
night,' she added, sliding an affected look of guilt at the children.
'Will you tell people about me?'

Max smiled at her uncomfortably.

'I don't know anyone, you know.'

Virginie's expression hardened. Paulo and Garance stood with their hands on their hips, their chins in the air, and a sinister look in their eyes, they looked ready to pounce.

'I don't have anything. No means of income,' the young woman said threateningly.

Max took a second envelope from his pocket.

'Here,' he said, 'I'd completely forgotten. It's for the children. Well, I mean, I decided that if I was really pleased I would give you a little bonus.'

It was Paulo who held out his hand.

'Put it in the drawer,' Virginie murmured.

The child obeyed her solemnly.

'I'll mention you at my club,' said Max to buy his freedom. 'I'm sure my bridge partners will be interested.'

The children disappeared immediately. He had spoken the magic words.

As soon as they were alone, Virginie let herself drop into a chair and put her head on her crossed arms. She shuddered to the rhythm of her sobs.

Max moved closer to her and put his arm round her shoulders. He sat next to her and stroked her head.

'And your parents? Can't they help you?' he whispered.

'I can't ask them for anything,' she replied between two spasms. 'They've got their own problems.'

Max thought about *matriochkas*, those Russian dolls that fit into each other from the smallest up to the biggest. It was the order of things.

'It's going to be all right, my dear,' he said in his most reassuring voice. 'You've got so much energy. You've done a good piece of work. You're a wonderful mother. If only all the children in the world had mothers like you.'

Virginie lifted her head, dry-eyed.
'Do you really think so?'

When Max left Virginie's house he turned left down the rue du Château-des-Rentiers. As soon he was sure he was out of sight he quickened his step to look for a big rubbish bin. As he was about to put the package on top of the plastic bags, he was overcome with anxiety: what if the bin happened to fall over as Virginie was walking past it? It looked stable enough, planted on its large rear wheels, but it could quite easily be knocked over by a car that had misjudged a manoeuvre.

He imagined the scene. Virginie nips out to do some shopping, she's distracted – probably thinking about the portrait, the first one she's sold – she doesn't see the car reversing to park. At the last minute she steps aside, crying out in surprise, the driver swerves and knocks the dustbin which tips over and spews onto the pavement the package that she had wrapped an hour earlier.

Max thought better of it and continued on his way. He did have to get rid of this burden, though.

He felt a sort of fear mixed with disgust at the thought of holding to him Telma's crushed head, her face which had been massacred by the young woman's incompetence. He was haunted by the image. A dying person's last wishes are sacred; Max had not respected his wife's.

Telma knew how to make her feelings clear: she preferred the idea of consumption by fire, which was clean and definitive, to that of a slow and hazardous decomposition. What had he hoped for? Virginie, like the good apprentice philosopher that she was, had unwittingly pursued the truth; from the ambiguous specifications she had managed to extract the hidden evidence: her portrait of Telma was, more than anything else, the portrait of a corpse. Despite paying belated homage to the debutante artist's clairvoyance, Max made a decision: to burn, he would have to burn everything, this one and the others, in a great heap on the balcony, a private auto-da-fé.

When he arrived home, he rang Angus then Frédéric and Marion, so as to complete his harvest. He had to be done with it as soon as possible.

When he was little his grandmother used to send him to sleep by telling him stories about the Maharal of Prague and his Golem. She had her own particular interpretation of the legend; according to her, the creature was a kind of Pinocchio. She was more inclined to emphasise the mistakes of this clay giant – which she regarded as an impetuous child – than the mystic teachings that most people drew from the parable. Every day she would invent a new blunder and, in her version, the Rabbi Yehouday spent his time running through the streets and dashing backwards and forwards across the fields and even the oceans, in his efforts to prevent his puppet from getting itself into trouble. Max remembered in detail the evenings he had spent on his grandmother's knee with his eyes half closed and his ears out on stalks, imagining the old man in a black coat, trotting along day and night, following in the footsteps of his idiotic great doll. He now found himself in a similar state of emergency.

With his heart in his mouth, he feverishly calculated how long it would take him to gather together the sacrilegious paintings, and he wondered how he would manage to get rid of them. If he'd taken the time to think calmly about the situation, he could only have laughed about it. But he was in a hurry, anxious, tormented by a childish fear, a fear of ghosts that he had never lost. That was what the painters had failed to understand.

Max wrung his hands, his breathing was laboured. He had spoken to each of them about the little twinkle in her eye, and on all three occasions this had been greeted with nothing but dull indifference. 'What I want,' he had specified, 'is that little look that she has, well, that she had. You can't really see it in the photos, that's why I'm telling you about it. The little light in her eyes. Do you see what I mean?' That's right, Grandpa, you keep chatting. He could have eaten them for breakfast. How can you accept a commission when you haven't grasped all the conditions? Bunch of crooks. They'd cheated him, out of greed, for the money, yes, that was it; all they wanted was his money. If they'd been serious artists, they would have refused. What was the point of all the endless discussions on history of art, the Umbrian School and working on distilling an instantaneous moment? If they knew so much about it, how had they missed the most important thing, this technicality? They had confused him with all their talk, to impress him, or to humiliate him even. Because how much more did they know than him, after all? Angus was just a psychotic who made fun of Diane. The lure of young flesh. She was at least fifteen years younger than him. It was easy to reel in something as ugly as that and, in the evening, with a pillow over her head – what the eye doesn't see the heart doesn't grieve – love could be blind from the neck up. And those little youngsters who didn't know anything. 'Did you do the Holocaust?' He'd let that go. Such idiots! What did they do during their history lessons? Doodle? Chairs on the ceiling. He should have taken that as a warning. They were mad. They'd made fun of him with their angelic faces and their pretence of innocence. We're just friends. Well, that was a rotten trick. It's unhealthy.

Once he had put Virginie's painting on the balcony, Max left the apartment, furious. In the end, Virginie was the only one who had proved to be honest. She had told him everything, hadn't tried anything on to sell her wares. Two children to look after and not a penny to spare, that was the limit of her technique. He would arrange to have some flowers and some presents for the children sent to her. As for the others, they'd asked for it.

'Is Diane not here?'

'Hello, Max, how are you?'

'Very well, thank you. How much do I owe you?'

'You don't seem yourself. Come in, sit down, please.'

'I'm quite happy standing, but I'm in a bit of a hurry. If you give me the painting I'll settle up and then I must go.'

Max drummed his fingers on one of the envelopes that he had prepared. Angus stood with his arms hanging limply by his sides and stared at him, dumbfounded.

'But it's not ready,' he said awkwardly.

'Well, why didn't you say so on the telephone, then?' said Max.

'I had no idea you wanted to take it.'

'Perhaps you thought I was coming for a cup of tea?'

Angus was right, Max was not his usual self. His brain was boiling between his temples. His nerves were so on edge they threatened to give way. He knew he was going too far, that there was no need to be so aggressive, but he couldn't help himself, and he felt a sudden flash of sympathy for all those inoffensive people who commit the most appalling crimes of passion.

'Diane told me that you came while I was away and, it's true, I thought you just wanted to come round to pay us a visit. It takes time to do what you have asked me to do, it's not easy.'

'Ah, so you admit it now. But it's too late. It'll have to be unfinished. It's very chic to do unfinished work. Tell me how much it is and you can count it amongst your award-winning works: unfinished portrait of the madman's wife.'

Max came a step closer and Angus backed away. The old man didn't take his eyes off the painter. He wanted to hurt him. A ball of anger was welling up deep inside him.

Angus suddenly turned his back on him. He shrugged his

shoulders and walked across the studio. What's come over me? thought Max. He really liked Diane, and Angus had been friendly towards him. Why did he have to destroy everything? He wasn't the aggressive type. He'd always thought that it was pointless to raise one's voice and, until now, he had never found a cause worthy of waking his rage. He didn't go to pieces if he was confronted with stupidity, hatred or injustice. He turned away, blocked his ears and went on his own sweet way. Was that out of weakness? Who could tell? Because he expected little from people and things, he was rarely disappointed.

Given the scale of the tempest, the density of the rancour that possessed him, he ended up thinking that his character must always have been tempered by an infinite wisdom: if I get angry, I kill. He must have realised this very early on. Now that he no longer had any strength, the barrier was falling and the toothless old lion had been released into the city.

'I'm sorry, Angus,' he said in a gentler voice. 'I've wasted your time.'

The painter turned round smiling.

'Who knows?' he said, coming over towards Max with a sheet of paper in his hand. 'I personally have no regrets.'

The old man leant against the wall and closed his eyes. He put his hand on his forehead and felt his legs buckling. A shadow passed over him.

'Are you feeling all right?' asked Angus, rushing over to support him.

'I'll be fine,' murmured Max. 'I'm sorry. How much do you want?'

He held out the envelope with a trembling hand.

'I don't want anything,' replied the painter. 'I warned you. I don't take commissions from individuals.'

Max took a deep breath and made his way to the door.

'Don't you want to take it?' said Angus with the portrait in his hand.

Max turned round, hesitated for a moment and took the sheet of paper he was offered.

'It's barely a sketch.'

The old man smiled painfully. An oval shape drawn in red chalk and criss-crossed with sketchy lines like those that one finds on the palm of a hand, a thin thread of a mouth, the top of the face veiled behind fine cross-hatching, with just one kiss curl, clear-cut in the middle of the forehead, emerging from the orangy fog.

'Thank you,' he said before hurrying out.

Once he was out in the street and blinded by the sunlight, he remembered that he had forgotten to ask for the photographs back. What did it matter. In thirty or forty years' time, some children would find the photographs as they rummaged through old cardboard boxes: 'Who's this lady?' they would ask. 'Probably a great aunt,' their parents would reply, not daring to throw them away.

When he reached Frédéric and Marion's apartment, Max was appeased. He waited a few minutes before ringing the bell, to catch his breath. His knees were hurting. The tense nerves in his back tightened into a ball as he arrived at the third floor. He was getting too old for this sort of expedition.

It was the boy who opened the door to him, with the reddened eyelids of someone who has just rubbed their eyes too vigorously.

In less than ten minutes the business was in the bag, a noisy plastic bag which still housed a few crumbs and a till receipt. The youngsters had counted the money in amazement while Max contemplated the collage. Marion had constructed a patchwork from fragments of painted photographs. She had drawn two great circles of gold around the eyes. Telma was beginning to look like an owl. Round her face, shimmering buds combined to form a strangely luminous garland. Max couldn't help himself smiling. It was really pretty, very jolly, a pagan icon in a crazy combination of colours. When he had offered to pay, Frédéric and Marion had politely refused, reminding him of the terms of the deal. 'I would like to,' the old man had said, begging them to accept this last whim of his.

'How do you like it?' Frédéric had asked with lowered eyes.

'It's very, how shall I put this?'

Max had lapsed back into his initial shyness. His mind, momentarily cleaned out by anger, was once again cluttered and awkward.

'I thought of an angel,' said Marion. 'When my grandmother died they told me she went up to heaven. I was eight. When you're little you believe everything you're told. The thing that worried me about that idea, though, was imagining everyone who'd died piled up up there, every time I looked up in the air. My father explained that space was infinite. I couldn't see what difference that made. So I imagined that when the dead went up to heaven they became minute, smaller than microbes. When I saw bits of dust moving in rays of sunlight, I told myself that my grandmother might be amongst them; that's completely ridiculous seeing as a bit of dust is much bigger than a microbe.'

She stopped talking, disturbed that the reasoning to which she had adhered for fifteen years had suddenly proved itself to be unreliable.

Frédéric was watching her, amused.

'And you, young man,' said Max, 'what do you think?'

'Of what?' asked Frédéric, a bit arrogantly.

'What do you think happens to the dead?'

The young man ran a hand through his hair and took a deep breath while a stubborn, childish pout twisted his handsome face.

'They're reincarnated,' he blurted eventually. 'No heaven, no hell. They could be a radish, a pigeon, a woman, a man, a pebble.'

'A pebble, really?'

'Why not, people once used to think the Earth was flat when it actually isn't.'

Max frowned, he didn't feel up to conducting this sort of debate.

'I'll leave you,' he said.

'Come back and see us,' said Marion, holding out her hand to him.

'I'd love to,' said Max. 'It's really very, very pretty,' he said shaking the plastic bag which held the third portrait.

Marion and Frédéric were watching him, half moved and half dismayed.

As he closed the door behind him, Max felt as if he were letting his own tombstone fall. Was it possible not to distinguish between a human and a pebble? Stones don't die, he thought. How could Frédéric ignore this evidence? He himself was immortal, that was why, Max told himself as he made his way to the bus stop.

Back home, he arranged the three portraits in a pyramid on the tiled floor of the balcony. He probably had some regrets about Marion's, but he didn't have any choice. He went to find the box of matches from the kitchen and knelt painfully in front of his pyre.

Before setting it alight, he briefly swept the horizon to check that no one could see him. He lived on the thirteenth floor of a tower block, and the school playground below was empty. He had another half hour before the end of lessons. When he looked up he saw the trails of weeping ivy that hung down from the balcony on the fourteenth floor. What would happen if the flames started licking at these leaves that had been dried out by the heat?

The fire might catch Mrs Zurcharelli's plantation and, from there, it might climb up all the floors to the top of the building. A towering inferno, no less. Get a hold of yourself, he told himself. We're not out in the country here. Fires are banned in the city, even in fireplaces. He would have to find another solution.

The rubbish chute was tempting, but Max suspected that Mr Rougier, the caretaker, might root through the rubbish. He was an extremely miserly man who had been wearing the same thread-bare suit for ten years and who claimed his new year's tips with all the ardour of a creditor.

He spread the three portraits out in front of him to study their chemical composition. Angus's had the advantage of being drawn on paper, it could easily be torn up. For Marion's collage, you could always use a solvent or methylated spirits, it was worth a go. As for Virginie's masterpiece, it seemed indestructible, it was so thick. A whole can of turps wouldn't get to the bottom of it. Max shuddered, he felt that he himself was infinitely more vulnerable. He would only have to get over the balustrade and it would all be over. We are powerless when faced with inanimate objects, he thought.

This thought plunged him into a long aimless daydream after which he stacked up the portraits and stowed them on the floor of the box room. That was the end of his story.

Lying on the sofa with his eyes still closed, he heard Nina going into the bathroom. The water ran for a moment. A clicking of combs and pins, the clunk of a glass put down on the porcelain shelf, the scant echoes of her secret, nocturnal ablutions. Through his closed eyelids he could sense the lights in the corridor, the bathroom and the bedroom going out one by one.

His eyes weighed heavily in their orbits, two marbles in a silk scarf. His temples widened, his shoulders spread; his hands, which he had crossed over his tummy, soon let go of each other: when his fingers had untangled themselves, the right hand rolled slightly to one side to come to rest against the backrest, while his left hand slipped past his flank to the edge of the sofa. This didn't stop its fall: it carried on falling into space and was held just one centimetre above the carpet by an arm that had lost too much of its suppleness to extend any further.

A large door opened. Max, in his dream, went in.

The incandescent light of an unexpected day whitened the walls of a long corridor at the end of which a clean-shaven old man with sparse white hair was sitting on a folding stool waiting for him. He was stocky with a very straight back and his knees slightly apart, and he watched him with his round black eyes. Max thought: 'Who are you?' A concert of voices answered him in various languages which he could not identify. 'You're the painter,' Max translated. The old man nodded.

There was an easel in front of the two men, Max sat down next to his host. The latter indicated the blank canvas and started to snigger.

'What's the matter?' asked Max.

'I had a feeling of *déjà vu*, that's what it's called, I think,' replied the other.

Max shrugged his shoulders.

'It's a cliché if you prefer. The painter confronted with his blank canvas, that's enough to make you laugh, isn't it?'

Max smiled hesitantly, and then burst into a forced laugh; he absolutely had to give a good impression.

'I'll recap,' said the painter. 'So there's Telma with her face, a pretty woman, I don't need to spell it out for you.'

He sniggered again and took a bouquet of paintbrushes, pencils and spatulas from his pocket.

'Choose a card at random!'

Max didn't understand.

'It's a joke. Take whatever you'd like. Go on, don't be frightened,' he added, waving the fistful of utensils under Max's nose.

'I wouldn't dare,' replied the latter with lowered eyes. 'It would be . . . how can I put this?'

'Sacrilegious? That is the word you wanted, or am I wrong? Don't tell me you're getting into all that. We all have a right to make mistakes, and that should save us from that sort of precious attitude. Go on, my friend. Don't be shy. You're the best person to choose, after all.'

Max felt himself lifting slightly off the ground, as if he were being transported on a cushion of air, and he ended up just in front of the canvas.

'Are you convinced now?' asked the painter. 'I'm joking. Who could do this portrait better than you? Because you loved this woman, didn't you? Photos are all very sweet, but you know as well as I do that they're at fault here. They're distorting mirrors, they give the illusion of a presence, they're like ghost traps, something you'd buy in a joke shop. They're not serious. Concentrate, Max. You can see her again. All it takes is for the letters of her name to appear in the right order and a picture of her comes to you immediately. She swirls round inside your head from every angle, in profile, full-on, from above, sitting, lying down, smiling, sad, young, old, naked, clothed. Here, take this to start off with, it's perfect.'

Max took the brown-coloured pencil that the painter offered him.

'There, that's right. Now, lift your hand, think of her and you're away. It couldn't be more simple.'

Max let his arm fall back down by his side.

'You're making fun of me. I can't draw a thing. It's not my job. You're the painter.'

153

'Being a painter isn't a job. Half the time I forget what painting means. If I knew how to paint, why would I paint? Of the two of us, you're better at this than me, admit it. As we're talking now, I haven't a single idea in my head, my mind is like the virgin territory of a newborn baby's. Whereas you! Fifty years of a face, the same face, not to mention the body that goes with it, the voice, the smell and everything. You're full to bursting with it. Get on with it, for goodness' sake.'

Max had fully made up his mind to get up. To ditch this joker, this crook, this good-for-nothing who was making fun of him. But his legs were not working.

He lifted his hand again and poked the canvas with the tip of his pencil. The lead sank into the creamy white fabric between two cross-threads, bore into it gently, embracing its soft texture. In the tunnel of bones a translucent tide ebbed away. Sparkles of crystal and rushing fibres sped from his shoulders to the back of his head, from his backbone to his heels. Max felt his body sloughing off its weight, rising up slowly, curved like that of a bird poised to catch the wind. A smile rose to his lips as he saw himself gliding head-down two metres above the ground.

Suddenly he fell back down.

'So, you see why I said it isn't a job.'

During his fall, Max had let go of the pencil. When he bent down to pick it up he saw, but he didn't understand, that the wood and the lead were being reduced to dust.

'Good materials make a good workman,' said the painter, handing him a paintbrush.

'I thought it wasn't a job.'

'Who said anything about a job? The workman in question is doing a piece of work. Don't get everything muddled up. You know much more about this than you're prepared to say. And this work consists of. . . .'

'It consists,' continued Max, who was possessed by his host's voice, 'of reassuring oneself that the world exists. You make a mark, you copy things out. Plagiarising the world confirms for us that the world is there.'

'Well, well,' interrupted the painter whose voice had returned to his own chest, 'let's calm down, my friend. Reassuring oneself that the world exists. There's nothing more to add. The more you say on the subject, the more inaccuracies you are likely to produce. Reality escapes our judgement.'

Max frowned. He was subject to a strange intuition. Who was this stocky little man built like a toad and with such piercing eyes, who was he really? He looked like . . . let's see . . . Oh yes, actually, it was striking: Picasso.

After taking a deep breath, Max opened his mouth, he had quite decided to unmask him.

'I've got it,' he cried. 'I know who you are!'

'It was well worth shaving my beard and leaving my chair of clouds at home,' replied the painter.

'I feel much better,' said Max, giving himself a shake.

He stretched. He closed his eyes for a moment and then opened them again, he was blinded all over again by the brightness of the light and he felt his hand being lifted by a winch that used his sorrow as a counterweight, and heading for the centre of the canvas with the paintbrush pointing forwards.

'All I want, Telma, is to talk to you once more. To ask you two or three questions. To know what you think.'

'But I don't exist any more.'

'I know. I've understood that.'

The surface of the canvas was smooth and shiny, it rippled slightly before stretching itself even further until it was as transparent as glass. When the paintbrush skimmed over it, it solidified completely into a funereal marble so polished it was like a mirror.

The face appeared with extraordinary clarity although it was intermittent.

'Are you smiling?' Max asked.

'No.'

'Why?'

'I don't know.'

'You were never happy.'

'That's what you wanted to believe.'

'The past, always the past. And when it wasn't the past it was the future, the children's future, the grandchildren's.'

'The present was you, and I loved you enough. That's not a bad start, you know?'

'What was the point of all that scorn, my poor little wife? What wouldn't you have done to have given yourself some importance? I loved you enough, too. Perhaps even a bit more. Just to annoy you.'

'Leave me alone now. Let me go.'

'Never. I'll hold on to you till the end of time.'

'If you resent me for so many reasons, why did you stay? You could have left me. It does happen.'

'You were the one who was leaving. All that looking into corners, all those muttered sentences. Do you think I was blind and deaf?'

'It's too late to make me over again. I've been un-made for now.'

'You won in the end. It was you who left me.'

'Hardly.'

'I won't force you to admit it. You won't leave me alone. Not a moment's peace. You're prowling round me. You're torturing me.'

'Because that's what you really want. I'm not doing so badly where I've ended up.'

'Better than with your idiotic husband, that's for sure.'

'Why not? At least I'm free.'

'Nonsense. When are you going to get down off your pedestal?'

'Never. I'd rather die.'

'Very funny. I didn't know you had a sense of humour.'

'There are so many things you don't know.'

'Go on, carry on. Humiliate me. Drag me through the dirt as you always did. You wouldn't know how not to. You're an automaton; not an ounce of heart in you.'

'Why do you say that? You'll regret it later.'

'I say that for all the things you didn't say to me.'

'I don't understand what you're talking about.'

'The children.'

'Leave the children out of this.'

'I'll do without your advice for once. The children are fine as they are, that's not the point.'

'What are you getting at then?'

'You never told me they looked like me. You never told anyone.'

'So?'

'So I hate you. I could stick a knife between your eyes. And even that wouldn't be enough. I need to go on and lacerate your face. And cut off your smile. And open up your eyelids.'

'Why did you stay?'

'Your vampire's appetite is never going to be satisfied is it? If I stayed it wasn't because of your intelligence; I could have done without that. It wasn't for your looks; you were never my type, flat-chested with grasshopper legs, a real skeleton. The only thing that connected me to you – I don't even know whether you'll be able to understand this because in order to understand it you'd need some guts – the only thing was your smell. The smell of your skin, your body, your mouth. I'd never smelt anything like it. Unbelievably sweet. However angry I felt, I just had to move towards you. By the time I was a metre away, I would already be quivering. I could have put my hands round your neck to strangle you and your smell would have disarmed me. You're a nasty woman, Telma. You always have been. But your smell is sweetness itself. You can't do anything about it, and neither can I.'

A tear rolled down Telma's silent face which disappeared just as it had appeared.

'What are you doing?' asked the painter.

Max waved his arms in a haphazard way; the random brush-strokes left invisible marks on the canvas.

'I'm begging her to forgive me,' he replied.

'That's unworthy of you.'

'Really?'

'You can do better than that.'

'Do you think so?'

The painter evaporated without giving a reply.

Max got up. He took his penknife out of his pocket and, one by one, he pulled the nails out of the frame. When the canvas was released it sank to the floor. Max straightened it out, weighed it up. It was white and supple like a sheet. That last piece of their wedding trousseau. He lay himself down on the ground, grabbed it and spread it over his body. 'Come and lie down next to me,' he whispered. Telma was as fluid as a breath of air, she stroked his ear one last time and dissipated into the atmosphere.

When he woke up Max smelt a delicious aroma of coffee.

'Did you sleep well?' asked Nina.

'Like the dead,' replied Max. 'And I won't insult you with an account of my dreams. I don't remember anything.'

They sat at the kitchen table, nibbling pieces of toast, informal and happy.

'You worked very late last night, didn't you?' he asked.

'Don't make a thing of it, I won't show you anything.'

'Why not? Are you ashamed of it.'

'No. That shows how little you know me. I've known for a long time that being ridiculous can't kill you. It's not that. If I tell you, you won't believe me. And if you believe me, I'll think you're stupid.'

'Well, that's never killed anyone, either.'

'You're more the scientific type, aren't you?' asked Nina, filling Max's cup.

He had never thought of it in those terms and was not at all sure how to answer.

'What I mean by that,' she continued, 'is that you have a rational sort of mind. You're a sceptic. I believe what I see.'

'I believe what I see,' Max repeated to himself, disconcerted.

'You're going to laugh, but never mind. I'll tell you everything if you swear you won't tell Mr Jacques any of it. He doesn't like this sort of business. He wouldn't have thought twice before burning the witches. Do you see the sort of person I mean?'

Max couldn't help himself delighting in the least dig at the man who, without anyone daring to admit it to themselves, was becoming his rival.

'When you went to sleep, I set to work. First thing, the shape of the face, the chin, the forehead, then the position of the eyes. You'd be amazed to know how much that can vary. Some people have close-set eyes like a mouse, others have them wide apart like a cow or an elephant. Then I make a note of all the significant distances: between the nose and the mouth, between the eyebrows, the little architectural details which make each face unique. As far as you know, your wife had beautiful proportions.'

'I never really noticed,' said Max.

'I can imagine, but, looked at in detail, it's even more striking.

When I'd finished my little bit of geometry, I attacked the colour. For each painting, I define a series of tonalities which seem to me to correspond with my subject. It was fairly obvious in this case. Browns, ochres, a tiny bit of mauve for the eyelids and a bit of green for the hollows of her cheeks. I was away. You should have seen me! I couldn't sit still.'

Nina smoothed her short hair with both of her elegant, bony hands.

'I was sure it was going to work. I'd decided to paint her with her scarf on, like in one of the photos. It's so pretty and timeless. Say that that's how you'd like to see her. I'm sure of it. I'm excellent at telepathy. Say it.'

She was jumping about on her chair with clenched fists.

'It's true,' said Max after a time during which he revelled in his hostess's childish excitement.

'I knew it. I could tell. I was in such a state. It hadn't happened to me for years. The night was completely black and silent around me. You could have told me I was about to change lead into gold and I wouldn't have been in any more of a fluster. Do you have moments like that? I'm sure you've experienced something like it. You're the only person in the world who's awake and everything seems possible. A night of love can be like that. Are you smiling? I warned you that it was ridiculous. But promise me you won't make fun of me.'

'I swear,' declared Max. 'If you want I could even cry.'

'I wouldn't ask that much of you. It must have been at least one o'clock in the morning when I started my first sketch. Sometimes the first one gets it right, but I'm always wary. I always stack a pile of paper in front of me, just in case. If I don't feel it, I screw up the top sheet of paper and start again.'

Nina stopped and sighed, glancing skywards.

'This is where the plot thickens,' she announced to Max who

was staring at her, frowning. 'I put my left hand absolutely flat on the paper and I started to draw the oval outline. I'd hardly gone two centimetres when my right arm became terribly stiff. I thought it was cramp and I let my arms fall down by my sides and took lots of deep breaths. It's the sort of little discomfort that happens at our age. The constriction eased up and I set back to work. This time it felt as if I were dragging an anvil across the page. My hand barely had the strength to hold the pencil. It was so heavy that I couldn't control it. I was about to give up when suddenly. . . .'

'A genie came out of the lamp!' Max exclaimed, laughing.

'You swore. You won't feel like making fun in a minute, I can promise you.'

'I'm sorry.'

'It's the last time, I'm warning you.'

Max gratified Nina with a military salute which made her smile in spite of herself.

'So, I was saying that suddenly my hand started to squeeze the pencil with more strength than I've got in the whole of my body. My joints started going white. I tried to let go, but none of my fingers seemed to be obeying me. That's when I witnessed the most extraordinary spectacle. Under my very eyes, the pencil set to work incredibly quickly, so violently that my heart started going like a train and I had trouble breathing, drawing a face that I know only too well. Nothing like my usual style. I do shadows with simple straight-line shading, the portrait that my hand was carrying out is covered in cross-hatch shading. I like to keep all the outlines in the same thickness but, in front of my own eyes, a straight line gave way to stippling, and pencil marks that were finer than baby's hair. My elbow was sweeping from left to right and top to bottom. How long can this have gone on, a minute, an hour? All I know is that at the end I fell in a heap at the table and went straight to sleep.'

Who was it then that snuck to the bathroom before calmly switching the lights off, one by one? Max wondered. Probably a ghost.

'You see,' he said. 'I'm not making fun of you. You who complained that you never had any dreams. You've got what you asked for. Not everybody has that much imagination.'

'So, you don't believe me?'

'I'm terribly sorry,' said Max.

'But it's worse than that.'

Nina jumped to her feet and ran to her room as quickly as her high-heeled mules would allow.

'Here,' she said, handing him a sheet of paper, 'The proof,' she added breathlessly.

Victory! Max thought triumphantly. She was as easy to manipulate as a schoolgirl.

'Just as I said: a dream,' he said, stroking the untouched page.

'Turn it over,' said Nina who had still not caught her breath.

He obeyed her and had to conjure up his darkest memories in order to stop himself bursting out laughing. On the piece of paper, chopped and shaded in every direction, vigorous and incredibly lifelike, a face emerged in infinitely delicate shades of grey. But it was Nina's face.

'A great likeness.'

Standing in front of her, Max lifted the portrait and held it next to its author's face.

'And it's a very pretty picture,' he added.

Nina blushed, without realising that it was also because of the lie she had told.

Mathusalem

My dear son,

Some news from your father.

Who knows where and how decisions are made? I only hope that you won't resent me for this. I'm sending this letter by express mail so that you can at least prepare yourself psychologically for my arrival. I haven't said anything to your sister yet, I wouldn't put it past her to send an ambulance round for me.

I didn't know how to tell you this, but there it is, it's done. I'm leaving on the fourteenth. I've reserved my seat on a flight to La Paz with a stop off in Buenos Aires. There was another one that stopped off at Bogota, but that would have been an eighteen-hour journey. The young woman at the agency, who seems to me to know more about cardiology than most of the doctors I've seen in the last ten years, formally advised me against it. It's not worth coming to pick me up at the airport, I'll take a taxi. If you can't be free when I arrive, leave the keys with the caretaker. You do have a caretaker, don't you?

Actually, it's more complicated than I thought. You'll almost certainly have to ring me as soon as you've received this letter. Don't go thinking that I'm trying to save on the phone bill my end. It's just that I wouldn't have the courage to tell you all this out loud. I know myself too well.

To tell you what, incidentally? My mind is very muddled. You've no idea. I thought I'd found wisdom and I realize that I've gone mad. The young woman at the agency, still the same one, tried to reassure me. I think she knows less about psychiatry than cardiology but she's only paid to sell plane tickets, after all.

At first, when I told her that I wanted to go to Tokyo via La

Five Photos of My Wife

Paz, she laughed in my face. It didn't put me off. She probably gets dozens of jokers wasting her time every day, planning journeys that they'll never make. So, to soften her up, I told her my little story. I told her about you, Nadya and your mother. She knew exactly what I meant because she's about the same age as you two and it just happens that her parents still live in Algeria. (Her name's Yasmina, a pretty brunette with big dark eyes that protrude a bit from her face, do you know the type?)

She was very frank. She said this: 'Mr Opass, I won't disguise the fact that it will be very long, very expensive and very tiring.' I replied: 'Very long? That's all I want, at my age you only have one motto: so long as it lasts.' That made her laugh. 'Very expensive? What do you think I should do with my savings? I'm not rich enough for a pretty young woman like you to fall in love with me.' That made her laugh too. 'Very tiring? At worst it'll kill me and, when I get to heaven, I can always show off saying that, despite my eighty years, I didn't die of old age.' That only made her smile. It wasn't so funny and people don't like jokes about death, especially young people, it makes them feel guilty.

I know it's mad. But . . . how can I say this to you? Admitting to you what's been tormenting me seems far more exhausting and costly than any round-the-world trip. I'm doing what I'm doing for your mother, to honour her memory, but also for me. I've always wanted to visit you and Nadya. Now that I think about it, I can think of whole nights spent trying to appease the desire as if it had been an appalling itch. What held me back? That's what I find difficult to say and yet, you'll see, it's nothing, practically nothing.

When your mother was still alive, I preferred not to mention it to her. I told myself: if she wants to go and see the children, she'll tell me. If she doesn't talk about it, it means she'd rather they came here. When she disappeared I stopped wondering about it, as if the whole possibility had vanished with her.

I now know what was holding me back. It's nothing and it's everything. It's so stupid that I'm ashamed to say it. I was afraid that you wouldn't be pleased to see me. My mother died when I was three and my father when I was seventeen. I don't know what it's like to see your parents getting old. When you and Nadya left France I felt relieved. You would come back when you wanted to. I told myself that, like that, we would be less of a burden to you. You could open our door like a photo album which stayed shut the rest of the time.

Why've I changed my mind? I'll never know. All I can tell you, my son – what a legacy! – is that we don't know any more about it at my age than at yours. Everything that I've learned in eighty years would fit in the palm of a baby's hand. The only thing that counts is life. Besides that there's nothing, no mystery to go chasing, not a shred of enlightenment.

Call me when you get this letter. There'll still be time to cancel – given the price of the journey, that's the least of my worries. I miss your mother. She was my compass, the wind in my sails. Was I to her what she was to me? I can't begin to imagine what my life might have been if I hadn't spent it by her side? I was so indecisive. You've no idea, like a grain of pollen in the wind. You and your sister are all that's left of her for me, and all that's left of me. Forgive the old egotist that I am.

Your father who loves you.

Max had not taken the sleeping pills that Yasmina had recommended. When the hostesses had come along the aisles asking the passengers to lower the blinds over the windows, he had pretended to be asleep. The silky cravat of the uniform had tickled his cheek while a woman with a brutal smile and a tight chignon leant over him to execute the task. It was the curfew. The lighting had swung from daylight to muted evening light.

Max looked at his watch, it was quarter to midnight. The night-lights had gone out one by one while a few screens still glimmered before closed eyes many of which were hidden behind eye-masks.

Business Class, Max said to himself, slightly tipsy from the two glasses of champagne that he had had to accompany his foie gras. Having checked that no members of the on-board personnel were in sight, he carried out his plan. Very casually, levering himself with his right arm, he slipped towards the empty seat beside him. The aim was to manage to rest his head on the arm-rest so as to bring his eyes in line with the bottom of the plastic shutter. Once he was in the desired position, he executed a quarter turn and lifted the blind a few millimetres with his left hand. A flash of white, almost silver, light instantly streamed onto his retina. Victory. So it was true. The sun was still shining, the sun would go on shining until he arrived. He was on board the machine that turned back time. Two weeks in La Paz and, bingo, he would carry on in the same direction, heading for Japan, which wasn't called the Land of the Rising Sun for nothing.

How long will it be before I start getting younger? Max wondered.

When my hair and my beard have turned blond again and when my body has rediscovered its suppleness, I'll go home. 'Young and broke,' he thought. He had sunk his last centime into this aerial cruise. He scratched his head, raised the sliding blind again and smiled. He might not go back at all.